Ultimate Family Treasury

"Wilbur Takes Wing" and "Bianca and Bernard Down Under" feature characters
from the Disney film *The Rescuers Down Under* suggested by the books by Margery Sharp, The Rescuers and Miss Bianca,
published by Little Brown and Company and William Collins Sons and Company.

"Happy Birthday Dumbo" are based on the Walt Disney
motion picture Dumbo suggested by the story Dumbo, the Flying Elephant, by Helen Aberson and
Harold Perl. Copyright © 1939 by Rollabook Publishers, Inc.

"A Forest in Flames," "Friendship Blooms," and "A Slippery Situation" are based on the edition containing the full text
of Bambi, A Life in The Woods by Felix Salten, published by Simon & Schuster.

"The Trouble with Tiggers," "Missing: Christopher Robin," "Silly Old Bear," and "The Perfect Present for Eeyore"
are all based on Pooh stories by A.A. Milne

"Stick Together" are © Disney Enterprises, Inc./Pixar

This edition published by Parragon in 2011

Parragon
Queen Street House
4 Queen Street
Bath, BA1 1HE, UK
ISBN 978-1-4454-4022-4
Printed in China

Ultimate Family Treasury

Adapted by Sheryl Kahn, Ann Braybrooks,
Vanessa Elder
and Rita Walsh-Balducci

Bath · New York · Singapore · Hong Kong · Cologne · Delhi
Melbourne · Amsterdam · Johannesburg · Auckland · Shenzhen

Contents

Saving the Day: Stories About Courage and Responsibility

The Beauty Within: Stories About Fairness and Judgment

Journeys of Discovery: Stories About Happiness

Foreword

Ask a group of children about Dumbo, and listen to what they tell you. It wasn't right for the animals to ridicule the tiny elephant with the gigantic ears. Their cruel laughter and taunts hurt Dumbo, and he felt sad and all alone. A mouse became his best friend, even though everyone knows that mice and elephants don't usually get along. With the whispered encouragement of his friend, Dumbo learned that his liabilities were his assets; he flapped his huge ears and soared above those who had criticized him. No-one had ever seen an elephant fly, but then no-one had ever known an elephant like Dumbo. The story reminds us that it is not right to make fun of someone because he is different.

Talk to children who have watched *Beauty and the Beast* and in their own words they will tell you that hatred is hideous. Belle's true beauty was not found in her appearance, but in her willingness to offer her life for her father's, and in the transforming power of her love for the Beast. At first she was afraid of the ogre, but she treated him with kindness and the Beast became less beastly. Belle no longer saw him with her eyes, but with her heart. Her love transformed the Beast and helped us all to see that he always was a handsome prince.

Ruth, my preschool daughter, knows that it isn't right to hurt others. I hope she learned that lesson from her sister, mother, and me; however, she may have picked it up from *101 Dalmatians*. Ruth knows it isn't right to hurt those puppies just so Cruella DeVil can have a spotted coat. And perhaps she will come to realize the great power of Aladdin's final selfless wish. His ultimate hope was not for riches, wealth, or fame, but to set the Genie free and remove the shackles of oppression that bound his friend.

This book affords you and a child you love the opportunity to share simple stories, look at beautiful illustrations, and discover profound truths. As you sit on the couch side by side, or when a small head rests against your chest as you gently rock in a chair, or when the bedroom lights have dimmed in preparation for "good night," open this book. Share with a child a short story from the wonderful world of Disney, and together discover that we have a responsibility to love and care for others. Tell them the stories that remind us that life is not measured by what we perceive with our eyes or grasp in our hands, but what we see by faith and treasure in our hearts. After all, these are stories for children of all ages. May the children you love and the child that lives within you enjoy and learn from them.

Reverend Michael Catlett, Ph.D.
9 March, 1998

ON LAND AND AT SEA

STORIES ABOUT FAMILY

A Whale of a Tale

from *Pinocchio*

When you love someone, their life can mean more to you than your own.

To become a real boy, all the wooden puppet, Pinocchio, had to do was be brave, truthful and unselfish. But he was having trouble living up to any of those ideals. He had already lied to the Blue Fairy. And then he had been weak and selfish by going to Pleasure Island, where he had smoked cigars, played pool and almost been turned into a donkey.

Ashamed, Pinocchio swam back to the mainland with Jiminy Cricket. Outside Geppetto's workshop, Pinocchio cried, "Father! Father, I'm home!"

No-one answered. Geppetto was gone. And, from the look of the dust and cobwebs, he had been gone a long time.

As Pinocchio and Jiminy sat outside, a dove dropped a piece of paper at their feet. The note said

that Geppetto had gone looking for Pinocchio and been swallowed by a whale named Monstro. Apparently Geppetto was still alive inside the whale, which was resting at the bottom of the sea.

"I'm going to find my father," Pinocchio declared. "I'm going to the bottom of the sea."

On a high cliff, Pinocchio tied a heavy rock to his tail. Jiminy grabbed hold of the rope and plunged into the water with Pinocchio.

At the bottom of the sea, Jiminy grabbed a smaller rock to use as a weight. Pinocchio wandered into a school of fish and, before he knew it, he was swept into the whale's belly.

Pinocchio saw his father sitting forlornly in his fishing boat. "Father!" cried Pinocchio. "I've come to save you."

"No, Pinocchio. There's no way out. Monstro only opens his mouth when he's eating. Then everything comes in – nothing goes out."

Pinocchio thought hard. "Father! We'll build a big fire, and the smoke will make Monstro sneeze!"

They started a blaze with some of the wood from Geppetto's boat.

As the flames grew, Pinocchio and Geppetto hastily built a raft with the remaining wood.

The whale shook, then sneezed. The tremendous force sent the little raft hurtling out of Monstro's mouth.

The furious whale swam beneath the raft and thrust it into the air. Geppetto and Pinocchio tumbled into the sea. "Hurry, Father!" cried Pinocchio.

"I can't make it, son. Save yourself."

"No, Father, I won't leave you!" Pinocchio grabbed Geppetto's shirt and dragged him to shore. There was no way he was going to let his father out of his sight now.

Later, after both Pinocchio and Geppetto
were safely at home, the Blue Fairy rewarded
Pinocchio by making him into a real boy.
He had proven himself brave, truthful
and *unselfish*.

Stormy Night

from *The Old Mill*

―――― ⟨⟨⟨ ――――

Mothers protect their children. And sometimes miracles protect mothers.

In an abandoned windmill, a blue barn swallow accepted a worm from her mate. All day, she had been sitting on her nest, keeping her three eggs warm. Together she and her mate had built the nest in a cog hole of an old millstone.

The blue barn swallows were not the only animals who had made the mill their home. Bright-eyed bats clustered in the rafters. A plump old owl perched on a wooden beam. Often the barn swallows watched the owl fluff his feathers and swivel his head from left to right, right to left.

On this night, the barn swallow watched the bats unfold their wings and dart towards a hole in the side of the mill. For a moment, moonlight illuminated their ragged shapes. Then the moon disappeared behind thick clouds, and the bats faded into darkness. Her mate followed them into the night to look for more food.

Inside the mill it was quiet, except for the soft, occasional hooting of the owl. The barn swallow shifted on her nest. As she blinked in the darkness, she felt a cold wind blow through the chinks in the walls. Then the wind shook the mill and howled.

Rain started to fall. The drops fell one at a time, then pounded the roof in a steady rhythm. Water seeped in through holes in the roof, but did not drip onto the nest.

The wind shrieked loudly. Suddenly the mother swallow saw the huge mill wheel coming towards her. The wind had snapped the rope that held the mill wheel, and the arms of the old mill had begun to move, turning the wheel inside with them.

In fright, the swallow darted away from her nest. Then she flew back and sheltered the eggs with her wings. The big, heavy wheel rolled over her nest, but the swallow and her eggs escaped being crushed. The cog that matched the hole containing her nest was broken.

All through the night, the swallow remained on her nest to protect her eggs. When the storm died down, the windmill ceased to turn and the sun glowed through the many chinks in the old, abandoned mill. She was glad to see her mate return. He brought food for their newly hatched children.

Home, Sweet Home

from *Peter Pan*

There's no better way to end the day than with a kiss from Mum or Dad.

The Darling children had heard many wonderful stories about Peter Pan, but they never dreamed they would ever really meet him. So when Peter Pan flew into the nursery one night, they were delighted.

"Come with me to Never Land," Peter told Wendy, John and Michael. And so they did, flying through the night sky with him and his pixie friend, Tinker Bell.

Never Land was filled with all sorts of interesting people. The Lost Boys were Peter Pan's friends, and they were very excited that he had brought some new children to play with them.

"This is Wendy," Peter Pan explained. "And I've brought her here to be your mother."

Wendy shook her head. "I can't be their mother," she explained. "I still need my own mother too much."

None of the Lost Boys had mothers of their own any more. "What's a mother?" one of the Lost Boys asked Wendy.

Wendy felt very sorry for them. "She is a wonderful person who loves you very much," Wendy told them.

Peter Pan frowned. The Lost Boys seemed more interested in mothers than in playing pirates.

Wendy went on. "A mother tells you wonderful stories and kisses you good night at the end of the day."

"Are you our mother?" Michael asked Wendy.

"Of course not," Wendy said. "I'm your sister. Don't you remember our real mother?"

John picked up his hat. "I remember her, Wendy!" he cried. "And I propose we go home to her at once!"

Wendy, John and Michael said goodbye to Peter Pan and his friends. Never Land grew smaller and smaller as they flew through the sky towards home, where their own mother was just getting ready to kiss them all good night.

King Triton's Gift

from *The Little Mermaid*

A loving father cannot help but forgive.

King Triton was exuberant. Together, he and Eric had defeated the wicked sea witch, Ursula, and saved the merpeople from her evil schemes. But before he could rejoice, he had to find Ariel. He knew that his daughter would not be happy until she was reunited with her true love.

Triton hadn't approved of Eric, or of any humans for that matter. He had seen too many sea creatures caught by their cruel fisheaters'

hooks. But now he realized that Eric was different. Eric had risked his own life to save Ariel – and for that, Triton would always be grateful.

Sebastian and Flounder led the Sea King to the shore where Ariel was sitting on a rock. She was mournfully watching Eric as he lay unconscious on the sand.

Triton turned to Sebastian. "She really does love him, doesn't she?"

"Mmm," Sebastian agreed.

"Well then, I guess there's just one problem left," mused the King.

"What's that, Your Majesty?"

"How much I'm going to miss her."

Sebastian's jaw fell open. With a sigh, Triton raised his trident and sent a beam of magical light towards Ariel.

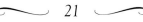

As Ariel looked down to see what was happening, she saw her fish tail being transformed into legs – human legs like she had always dreamed! She looked up and beamed at her father.

Eric began to stir. When he saw Ariel walking towards him out of the ocean, his face lit up. At last they were free! And they belonged to each other.

King Triton smiled sadly. He knew that he would not be able to see his remarkable daughter every day as he had in the past. But he was warmed by the knowledge that she would have a happy future with a man who loved her as much as he did.

A Forest in Flames

from *Bambi*

Your family is your most precious possession.

 careless hunter had forgotten to put out his campfire, and now the whole forest was ablaze. Bambi and his father tried to make their way through the burning trees, but as the wind changed direction, so did the fire.

Bambi's father used all his experience with forest fires to find a path through the blazing woods. As Bambi ran for his life, he felt stronger knowing that his wise father was by his side.

They ran through a stream, hoping the water would protect them from the flames. But the trees along the banks were ablaze, too.

At last Bambi and his father came to a waterfall. The trees behind them were burning. Trapped, they had only one choice: to jump.

They landed with a great splash. Exhausted, they swam slowly to an island in the middle of the river.

Nearby, Faline stood at the water's edge, looking up at the hills. She fearfully watched her forest burn. She, too, was weakened by fatigue, but she could not rest until she knew Bambi was safe.

As she listened and watched, she heard splashing. Two stags were walking towards her through the shallow water. As they emerged from the smoky haze, she recognized them.

"Bambi!" she cried.

Though he was very tired and sore, Bambi dashed through the water towards Faline's voice. He climbed up on the rock beside her. She was alive!

The deer stood close together and watched their forest burn. With heavy hearts, they realized that many animals would now lose their homes. They were grateful, though, to be safe and to at least have each other.

A New Home for Tod

from *The Fox and the Hound*

———— ∞ ————

Two lonely souls can make one happy family.

From her nest in the old oak tree, a wise owl called Big Mama witnessed the whole sad event.

She was just settling down for bed when a terrified mother fox burst out of the woods. The fox was carrying a newborn cub in her mouth.

She quickly hid her baby in the tall grass by a fence and then tore across the meadow, clearly running for her life. She was followed closely by a pack of baying hounds.

Moments later, Big Mama heard rifle shots. She knew that the baby fox was now alone in the world.

Big Mama flew down to the baby. "You poor little fella," she crooned, stroking his fur. He was shivering. "You're gonna need some carin' for."

The baby fox snuggled against Big Mama's soft chest.

"Oh, no! Not me, darlin'." Big Mama laughed. "But don't you move. Big Mama's gonna be right back."

She flew off in search of her friends Boomer and Dinky. She found them in a nearby tree, where they were trying to dig a stubborn caterpillar from his hole.

"Boomer!" Big Mama called to the woodpecker. "Stop that peckin' and listen. I need you and Dinky to help me."

She told them about the little fox and his mother.

"Gosh," said Boomer, "who'll take care of him?"

Dinky the sparrow ruffled his feathers.

"Hey! I got an idea!" he exclaimed. "The Widow Tweed is all alone. She'd probably be happy to take care of him. And I'll tell you how we'll arrange it . . ."

A few minutes later, the plan was hatched. Boomer tapped on the door of Widow Tweed's farmhouse.

"Yes?" the Widow Tweed called, opening the door and looking around. But there was no-one to be seen.

Just as she was about to close the door, Big Mama and Dinky flew down and plucked her pink underwear from the washing line.

"My word!" the Widow Tweed cried. "You come *back* here!"

She ran out of the house after the birds. They dropped her bloomers right near the fence.

As the Widow Tweed picked up her underwear, she was shocked to find a furry little animal huddled in the grass.

"Why, it's a baby fox," she whispered.

She bent down, and the tiny creature uncurled himself and tottered over to her.

Tears came to the Widow Tweed's eyes. "You're such a little toddler," she said, chuckling. "I think I'll call you Tod."

With that, she wrapped him gently in her apron and carried him inside.

As Plain as the Nose on Your Face

Stories About Honesty and Integrity

Bianca and Bernard Down Under

from *The Rescuers Down Under*

A small bump of goodness can topple a large evil.

In the Australian outback, a boy scrambled down the side of a cliff. A poacher, someone who caught and killed wild animals for money, had told him that his friend Marahute, the golden eagle, had been shot. Cody was devastated. He wanted to make sure that the eagle's eggs were safe.

Cody saw the eggs in the nest. "They're still warm!" he said, touching them gently.

As the boy covered the eggs with feathers, a lady mouse appeared at his side. "Cody!" she cried urgently. It was Miss Bianca from the Rescue Aid Society. Along with her partner, Bernard, and a kangaroo mouse named Jake, she wanted to warn Cody that the poacher, McLeach, and his lizard, Joanna, had followed him.

"There's no time to explain," Miss Bianca continued. "You are in grave danger."

Just then Cody saw the golden eagle flying towards the nest. "She's alive!" he cried. "Marahute! It's me!"

Bernard shouted, "McLeach is on the cliff!"

Above them, McLeach sat in his huge poaching machine with his pet lizard, Joanna.

"Marahute!" Cody cried. "Turn back! It's a trap!"

But it was too late. McLeach shot the net over Marahute and captured her. As the bundle swung from the crane, Cody leaped from the ledge and grabbed hold of the net. Jake lassoed Cody's foot and threw the end of the rope to Bernard and Miss Bianca. "Hold tight, you two," Jake cried. "We're going for a ride!"

Miss Bianca caught the rope, but Bernard lost his grip on it. The net swung away from the ledge without him.

McLeach pulled the net up with the crane. Then he dumped Marahute into the cage in the back of the truck, along with Cody, Jake and Miss Bianca.

As McLeach drove off, Bernard scrambled up the cliff and found a razorback boar to give him a ride. The boar sped off with Bernard on its back, and soon they caught up with McLeach's truck.

At Crocodile Falls, McLeach tied Cody to the end of the crane and dangled him over the rushing water. "You ready, boy?" McLeach cackled. "The crocs love live bait!" McLeach turned a key, and the crane began to lower the rope.

When McLeach wasn't watching, Bernard leaped into the truck and stole the key. The crane immediately stopped. McLeach grabbed his gun and began firing at the rope.

Bernard tossed the keys to Miss Bianca through a hole in the cage. Then he ran full speed towards Joanna and knocked her into McLeach. Both the poacher and the big lizard tumbled into the river. Joanna swam to the opposite bank, while McLeach was swept over the thundering falls.

The rope holding Cody suddenly snapped, and the boy fell into the river. Bernard dived in after him. Then, as Cody was swept over the falls, Marahute swooped down and caught them. On her back rode Jake and Miss Bianca. Thanks to Bernard, the captives had escaped.

The friends soared over the vast Australian outback, free at last.

Mickey's Magical Mix-up

from *The Sorcerer's Apprentice*

It takes a lot of learning to control a little magic – study hard.

Long ago, a powerful sorcerer agreed to take on an apprentice. Day in and day out, the sorcerer busied himself with his spells and incantations while Mickey did all the chores. As Mickey swept the floors, tended the fire and filled the vat, he dreamed of becoming a sorcerer. He knew he would make a fine magician, if only the sorcerer would stop for a moment and teach him a trick or two. The sorcerer had promised!

Late one night, the sorcerer placed his tall, pointed hat on the table and turned towards the stairs that led to his bedchamber. "When you've filled the vat with water from the fountain, then you, too, may go to bed," said the sorcerer.

"Yes, sir," said Mickey, watching him climb the stairs. Never before had the sorcerer forgotten his enchanted hat!

As soon as he was gone, Mickey ran over to the table and tried on the hat. Instantly Mickey felt that he, too, could make magic. The sorcerer need never find out.

Mickey spied an old straw broom in the corner. Using his newfound powers, he chanted, "*Dooma, dooma, brooma, brooma.*"

The broom sprang to life. Mickey commanded the broom to lift two buckets and follow him to the fountain in the courtyard. The broom filled the buckets with water and marched back to the vat. As soon as the broom finished, Mickey motioned for it to fetch more water.

Quite satisfied, Mickey sat in a comfortable chair and fell asleep. Soon he began to dream. Atop a pinnacle, surrounded by the sea, Mickey raised his arms to command the elements: fire, water, wind and earth. Shooting stars whirled around his head. The tides rose higher and higher until they splashed at his feet. He could almost feel the waves tickling his toes. . . .

Mickey awoke abruptly. He was sitting in waist-high water. All the time, the broom had continued to fetch the water and fill the vat, and now the room was flooded.

"Stop! Halt!" Mickey cried, but the broom continued. He searched for the sorcerer's book of incantations, but it had disappeared.

In desperation, Mickey grabbed an axe and chopped the broom into pieces. To Mickey's horror, the splinters sprang to life, each holding buckets. Blindly they marched to the fountain and back, filling the vat with water.

The room became a turbulent sea. When the missing book of incantations drifted by, Mickey climbed aboard. Frantically he turned the pages, trying to find a spell that would stop the brooms.

Suddenly the sorcerer threw open the door and murmured the incantation. The waters receded and Mickey sat, shamefaced, in a puddle. As the sorcerer glared at him, Mickey vowed that he would never make magic again . . . that is, until the sorcerer felt he was ready!

A New Scrooge

from *Mickey's Christmas Carol*

The more you give of yourself, the richer you become.

It was Christmas Eve. Bob Cratchit twisted his hands nervously as he faced his employer. Ebenezer Scrooge was never an easy man to deal with.

"A half day off!" shouted Scrooge in disgust. "For Christmas!"

Bob Cratchit looked down. This year seemed worse than ever.

"Go on," Scrooge finally said. "But be here earlier than ever the day after!"

That was how Ebenezer Scrooge treated everyone. He was the richest man in town, but had the coldest heart. Christmas meant nothing to him.

"Bah! Humbug!" Scrooge barked at anyone who wished him a merry Christmas.

That night, Scrooge heard a strange noise. "Who's there?" he called.

Suddenly, the ghost of his old business partner appeared. "It is I, Jacob Marley," the ghost said. "I've come to tell you that tonight you will be visited by three spirits."

Scrooge tried to ignore what the ghost had said. "Humbug!" he said. But as the clock struck midnight, the first spirit appeared.

"I am the ghost of Christmas past," he told Scrooge. Scrooge had no choice but to go with the spirit to see again how he had spent Christmas many years ago. Soon Scrooge saw old friends dancing and singing once more. He even gazed upon the face of Isabel, his old sweetheart.

Scrooge turned away. He knew that he had not been kind to Isabel, or any of the other people the spirit showed him. All he cared about was money.

Before long, another spirit came. "I am the ghost of Christmas present!" the ghost told Scrooge. Once more, Scrooge was carried out of his bed and into the snowy streets of London. He looked into the window of the tiny, poor home of Bob Cratchit.

The Cratchit family had little money, but endless amounts of love for each other. Scrooge was ashamed to think of how he had begrudged Bob time off to spend with his young son, Tiny Tim.

There was little time to think of that, though, for suddenly the final spirit appeared. "I suppose you are the ghost of Christmas yet to come," Scrooge said. In a puff of wind, he found himself in a lonely graveyard.

"Spirit, why do you bring me here?" Scrooge asked in a frightened voice. Then he saw a lonely tombstone before him – IT WAS HIS OWN!

Scrooge shouted, "I will change! I will be a better duck! I will keep Christmas in my heart all year long!" Then he realized he was awake and safe in his own bed. "It's Christmas!" he cried, jumping out of bed. He knew what he had to do. He ran over to Bob Cratchit's house.

"Merry Christmas!" Scrooge shouted as he pounded on the door. He had brought a huge bag of toys for the children.

"God bless us, every one," Tiny Tim said. And Scrooge couldn't have agreed more.

Mirror, Mirror on the Wall

from *Snow White and the Seven Dwarfs*

Jealousy of someone else's beauty only makes you more unattractive.

nce upon a time, a very beautiful but cruel Queen owned a magic mirror. Every time she looked into it, she asked the same thing:

> *"Magic mirror on the wall,*
> *Who is the fairest one of all?"*

The mirror always answered that she was the fairest in the land, until one day it replied:

> *"Famed is thy beauty, Majesty. But hold – a lovely maid I see!*
> *Alas she is more fair than thee!"*

The vain Queen knew at once that the mirror spoke of the Princess Snow White. The Queen vowed that the Princess must die.

Using her evil magic, the Queen transformed herself into an ugly old beggar woman. In her disguise, she went out to the forest where Snow White lived in hiding. Hanging on her arm was a basket of poisoned apples.

Snow White was not alone in the forest. She lived in the cottage of the seven dwarfs – Doc, Happy, Sleepy, Sneezy, Bashful, Grumpy and Dopey. They loved her gentle goodness and vowed to protect her from the wicked Queen. Each day, before they left to work in the

diamond mine, they warned Snow White to be careful.

Snow White knew that the Queen wanted to harm her, but she had no idea that the beggar woman who came to the cottage was her enemy! She kindly invited her inside.

"Hello, dearie," croaked the old woman. "Would you like to try one of my delicious apples?"

The forest birds and animals tried to warn Snow White, but it was too late. She took a bite of an apple and fell down in a deep sleep.

"Now *I* am the fairest in the land!" shrieked the hag.

The animals raced through the woods to the diamond mine. The dwarfs hurried back to their cottage and chased the wicked Queen up a mountain. Suddenly, a bolt of lightning struck the rock where the Queen stood, and she fell from the cliff, never to be seen again.

The dwarfs promised that they would never again leave Snow White's side. They stood guard beside her throughout the year, night and day until, one day, a young prince rode up.

The Prince recognized Snow White as the young woman he had once loved. Gently, he leaned over and kissed her. Snow White's eyes opened. The spell was broken at last!

Hook Hatches a Plan

from *Peter Pan*

Jealousy makes the heart smaller. Only love makes it grow.

Tinker Bell was a jealous little pixie. Her friend Peter Pan was spending all his time with his new friend, Wendy, and Tinker Bell was afraid he didn't care for her any more. Every time she tried to make that awful Wendy-girl go away, Peter foiled Tink's plan and rescued her.

If only that Wendy would just go away! Tinker Bell thought angrily.

At that moment, Captain Hook was trying to think of a way to be rid of Peter Pan forever. "If I only knew where his secret hideout was," he said. He decided to bring Tinker Bell to his ship and trick her into telling him.

"I will make Wendy go away forever," Captain Hook promised Tinker Bell. "But you must show me where Peter Pan lives so I can find her."

Tinker Bell happily showed Captain Hook Hangman's Tree on a map. With a delighted laugh, the evil pirate grabbed Tinker Bell and threw her into a lantern. Tinker Bell realized that she had been fooled, and now Peter was in danger!

"I won't lay a hook on Pan," Captain Hook promised. "This little present will do the job for me." Captain Hook sent a box to Peter Pan, and hidden inside was a bomb about to explode!

Tinker Bell knew she had to rescue Peter Pan. She pushed with all her might against the side of the lantern until it tipped over. Tinker Bell slipped out and flew as fast as she could to Hangman's Tree.

"Hi, Tink!" Peter called. "I was just about to open this present!"

Tinker Bell zoomed down, grabbed the box from Peter's hands, and whisked it away. Within seconds, the bomb exploded. Rocks and trees flew all about as the island shook from the blast.

"Goodbye, Peter Pan," Captain Hook said as he watched the explosion from his ship.

But Tinker Bell had saved Peter Pan. Just as the present exploded, she had pushed him to safety.

"Tink?" Peter Pan called. Under a big pile of rocks, a faint light glowed. "Tink, are you all right? You have to be all right! What would I do without you?" Peter Pan began to toss the rocks aside to rescue his dear friend.

Suddenly, Tinker Bell knew she had no reason to be jealous of Wendy. Peter Pan cared about her, after all. Knowing this, she began to feel better. Together the friends went off to foil Captain Hook's wicked plans once more.

The Queen's Quick Temper

from *Alice in Wonderland*

There's no pleasing some people. Try to avoid them.

Alice was quite lost. She had followed the White Rabbit down his rabbit hole, and from there on she had no idea where she was. No matter which way she went, the most unusual things happened to her. But she kept wandering through the woods until she heard some voices singing.

Perhaps they'll be able to tell me how to get home, Alice thought as she hurried into a formal garden.

Three gardeners were busy dabbing all the white roses on a tree with red paint. It was an odd thing for them to do, but Alice had seen many odd things on her journey.

"Why are you painting the roses red?" she asked them.

The three gardeners explained that they had planted white roses by mistake. The Queen wanted only red ones, and her temper was fierce. They were certain that she would chop off their heads if she found out.

"It's a wicked temper she has," they whispered fearfully to Alice.

"Oh, dear!" Alice cried. "Let me help you!"

Alice climbed a ladder and began to paint the white roses red, too. Suddenly a trumpet blasted. The Queen was coming!

Alice and the gardeners bowed down before the Queen. They trembled in fright as she approached. Just as they had feared, the Queen noticed the red paint at once!

"Who's been painting my roses red?" she roared. "The ace? The deuce? Off with their heads! Off with their heads!"

Everyone ducked as the Queen ranted and raged. Her face grew red and her loud voice echoed across the garden. Alice was terrified. She had never seen anyone with such a bad temper!

Just then the King, a meek little man, begged the Queen to let Alice and the gardeners have a trial. To everyone's surprise, the Queen agreed.

Alice watched in shock as the mischievous Cheshire Cat appeared. He winked at Alice. "Let's make her really angru, shall we?" he said with a grin.

"Oh, no!" Alice cried. The Queen's rage was even worse than she had imagined. Soon the Queen was shouting for everyone's head to be chopped off. It seemed there was no pleasing her that day.

Alice put her apron over her head to hide from the Queen's anger. In her pocket was a piece of the magic mushroom that had made her grow taller. Quickly she took a bite.

To the shock of everyone in the court, Alice grew and grew, right before their eyes.

"All people a mile high must leave!" shouted the Queen.

And so Alice left, running as fast as she could from the upside-down world of Wonderland and the Queen's quick temper!

The Small One

from *The Small One*

*When a creature has given all the work it can, you should repay it
with all the kindness you can.*

Long ago, there was a boy who lived near the town of Nazareth.
His father owned four donkeys to help with the chores. Three
of the beasts were young and strong, but the fourth, who was
smaller than the others, was old and weak. The boy took care of all
the donkeys, but he loved Small One best of all. Small One was his
friend.

One day, the boy and his father were gathering firewood. They
loaded the heavy logs on the donkeys' backs. The boy tried to find
the lightest pieces of wood
for Small One to carry,
for he knew that the
donkey was too
weak to carry a
heavy burden.

"Don't you
have enough
work to do
without doing
Small One's, too?"
his father asked.

"Oh, Father. He is no trouble at all. I don't mind," the boy said.

"Son," his father said. "Small One is old. His strength is gone. We cannot afford to keep him any longer."

The boy grabbed his father's arm. "No!" he pleaded. "You can't mean it!"

"Please, son," his father said, "try to understand. Small One is old. He should not have to work so hard. In town he will have an easier life. You must be strong."

"Yes, Father," the boy replied, but he felt as if his heart would break.

The little donkey, too, was very sad. But the boy tried to cheer him up.

"Don't worry, Small One," he said. "I won't sell you to just anyone. He will be someone special, someone who will love you as I do."

The next morning, the boy and Small One walked over the hills to Nazareth.

At the town gates they were stopped by a guard who demanded to know their business. "I have come to sell my donkey, sir," the boy explained.

The guard looked at Small One and laughed. "I know a man who is in need of such an animal," he said. "Go to the third shop inside these gates."

The boy thanked the guard profusely, but when they reached the shop, his heart grew cold. Inside, a man was sharpening a knife. Several animals were tied up, and they looked frightened.

The man offered the boy a piece of silver – for Small One's hide!

The boy and Small One ran away as fast as they could. "I'm sorry, Small One," the boy said when they were a safe distance from the tanner's shop.

From place to place they roamed, but no one wanted to buy Small One. Night was coming.

The tired donkey knew that only one man would buy him. He led the boy back to the tanner's shop, ready to give up his life to help his friend.

The boy sat down beside Small One and began to cry.

Suddenly, the boy felt a hand on his shoulder. He looked up into the eyes of a man.

"Tell me, son," the man said. "Is your donkey for sale? I need a gentle beast to carry my wife, Mary, to Bethlehem."

"Yes, sir," he said.

"What do you call him?" the man asked.

"Small One," replied the boy.

"Well, he looks strong enough," said the man.

"And kind," said the boy.

The man smiled. "I can offer you only one piece of silver," he said. "I know it is very little."

"Oh, that's fine!" the boy cried. "I just want Small One to have a good home."

"He will," said the man. "I'll take good care of him."

As the man, his wife and Small One disappeared down the road towards Bethlehem, the boy watched from a hilltop and waved goodbye.

The boy was sad, but also happy. For he knew that Small One had found a good home at last.

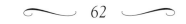

Marley's Mistakes

from *Mickey's Christmas Carol*

Bad deeds can come back to haunt you.

 ate one Christmas Eve, Scrooge made his way home. The wind moaned down the deserted streets and the snow swirled around him.

Scrooge reached his dark house and gazed up at the door. The knocker was carved in the shape of a lion's head. But tonight, it began to change right before his eyes!

The knocker looked exactly like his dead business partner, Jacob Marley! Scrooge couldn't believe his eyes. Suddenly an unearthly voice broke the silence. *"Ehhhbeneezer Scrooogе!"*

Scrooge looked around frantically. But the voice was coming from the knocker – from Marley's head!

"Jacob Marley?" Scrooge whispered. "No! It can't be!"

Scrooge yanked open the door and dashed inside. He ran up the stairs and into his bedroom. He slammed the door behind him and bolted all the locks. He heaved a sigh of relief. But a moment later, there was a loud knock on the door.

"Ehhhbeneezer Scrooogе!" the voice moaned again.

There was nowhere to hide. Scrooge pulled his hat down over his frightened eyes.

"Go away!" he cried.

But Scrooge could hear the sound of chains being dragged across the floor. He turned around and shivered to the bone. "Jacob Marley! It *is* you!"

"Ebenezer," the ghost moaned. "Remember when I robbed the widows and swindled the poor?"

For a moment, Scrooge forgot his fright. "Yes!" he cried. "You were brilliant!"

"No," said the ghost, "I was wrong. And so, as punishment, I'm forced to carry these heavy chains throughout eternity. I'm doomed!" The ghost waved its arms around in despair. "And the same thing will happen to you, Ebenezer Scrooge!"

"No!" Scrooge cried. "It can't! It mustn't! Help me, Jacob!"

But the ghost was deaf to Scrooge's pleas. "Tonight," it declared, "you will be visited by three spirits. Listen to them. Do what they say, or your chains will be even heavier than mine!"

And with that the ghost disappeared, leaving the miserable Scrooge shaking in his chair.

Poor, Unfortunate Souls

from *The Little Mermaid*

If you pick on someone weaker than you, your strength becomes your weakness.

Ursula was a sea witch who lived in the darkest corner of the sea, and she was as ugly as she was evil. For many years she had dwelt below the waves, tricking merpeople into giving up their souls.

Triton, King of the merpeople, had banished Ursula from his kingdom years ago, and she was bent on revenge.

One day, the demon gazed into her crystal ball, and she saw Ariel. Ursula sneered at the lovesick look on the girl's face. She now knew

the key to Ariel's heart. More than anything, Ariel wanted to be with Eric, a human.

"Oh, it's too easy!" Ursula sniggered. "The child is in love with a human. And not just any human – a prince! Her daddy will *love* that!"

Ursula threw back her head and cackled with glee. She danced around her collection of shivering, sad-eyed souls – all trapped in her garden of evil.

Each tiny, distorted body had once been a merperson – a merperson so fraught with desire that he or she had been willing to strike a deal with the evil Ursula. But the deals always ended in misery and unfulfilled dreams. Ursula saw to that, for she was anything but fair.

And Ursula vowed to add Ariel to her collection.

But Eric's love for Ariel was stronger than his fear of death. He attacked the powerful Ursula armed only with a harpoon. And though the Sea Witch let all her vast evil swell her to the size of a living mountain, Eric steered his battered ship straight at her, and its broken mast pierced her belly.

Ursula's cry of pain blotted out the sound of thunder. She sank like an island, disappearing forever. Ariel was free, and so were all the poor, unfortunate souls.

Dodger Sneaks a Snack

from *Oliver & Company*

A share of the work earns a share of the rewards.

ita, a leggy hound with long, silky ears, gazed sadly out of the window. Suddenly she brightened. "Here comes Dodger!" she cried. "Maybe he's had some luck."

A friendly mutt with a lopsided grin strutted into the shabby room. He was wearing a string of hot dogs around his neck. "Cool it, Dodger fans," he announced. "I'd like to introduce you to . . . dinner! Hot dogs à la Dodger!"

Francis the bulldog was so happy to see food that he could barely maintain his composure. "Thank you, Dodger," he said. "You remain our pre-eminent benefactor."

"Yeah, and you're okay, too," added Einstein, the gangly old Great Dane. "How did you do it?"

"Well," boasted Dodger, "let me tell you. It was tough! Only *I* could've done it. Picture the city – Eighth and Broadway. Crowds are hustling. Hot dogs are sizzling. Enter Dodger, one bad puppy. Then along comes a greedy, ugly psychotic monster with razor-sharp claws, dripping fangs and–"

Dodger's story was interrupted. An orange kitten fell through the rotting roof and landed in the middle of the dogs. The kitten was terrified.

"I – I followed a dog here," he stammered. "I . . . I just wanted some of the hot dogs I helped him get."

"Hey, kitty," Dodger said. "What took you so long?"

Francis sized up the kitten. "I assume this is the psychotic monster you were talking about."

"Come on, Dodger," jeered Tito the chihuahua. "Let's see this big, bad kitty in action."

Rita nuzzled the shivering kitten. "Enough messing around, guys. He's so little. I wonder where his mother is."

"You got a name, cat?" Tito asked.

The kitten shook his head. "I was left for adoption in a box. My brothers were all taken yesterday. Then Dodger came along. He said we'd be pals."

"We will be, kid," Dodger reassured him. "Now, dig in!"

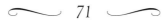

The Greatest Gift

Stories About Love and Friendship

The Trouble with Tiggers

from *Winnie the Pooh and Tigger Too*

You don't have to like everything about someone to love them just as they are.

Rabbit was tired of being bounced by Tigger – bounced and trounced and knocked down by Tigger. So he was quite happy when he and his friends found Tigger and Roo stuck up in a tree.

"Tigger can't bounce anybody as long as he's stuck up in that tree," Rabbit said cheerfully.

"We can't just leave them up there," said Christopher Robin. "We have to get them both down. Now, everyone take hold of my coat. Ready? Okay, you're first, Roo. Jump!"

"Here I come!" Roo cried, letting go of the branch. "Whee!"

Roo landed safely in the middle of Christopher Robin's coat. "That was fun!" cried Roo. "Come on, Tigger. Jump!"

Tigger frowned and clung tighter to his branch. "Jump? Tiggers don't jump. They bounce."

"Then why don't you bounce down?" said Pooh.

"Tiggers only bounce *up*," replied Tigger.

Christopher Robin sighed. "Then you'll have to *climb* down."

"Tiggers can't climb down because . . . because their tails get in the way." Tigger wrapped his tail around the tree trunk to prove his point.

Suddenly Rabbit came up with a solution. "If Tigger won't jump down or climb down," Rabbit proclaimed, "we'll just have to leave him up there forever!"

Tigger didn't like the sound of *forever*, but he said, rather sadly, "If I ever get down from this tree, I promise never to bounce again."

Rabbit did a little jig in the snow. "Did you all hear that?" he said gleefully. "Tigger promised never to bounce again!"

Tigger slowly unwound his tail from the tree trunk and looked down. With a bit of coaxing from his friends below, Tigger ever so carefully climbed down from the tree.

As Tigger stood in the snow, Rabbit reminded him, "You promised!"

"Not even one teensy-weensy bounce?" Tigger asked.

"Not even a *smidgen* of a bounce," replied Rabbit.

Tigger hung his head and trudged off into the woods, his tail dragging behind him.

Roo said to Christopher Robin, "I like the old bouncy Tigger best."

Christopher Robin agreed, as did Pooh and Piglet and Kanga. They all looked at Rabbit.

"Well, I . . ." Rabbit fumbled. Didn't his friends remember how annoying it was to be bounced by Tigger? It seemed not, because they all looked as droopy as Tigger.

"Oh, all right," said Rabbit. "I guess I like the old Tigger better, too."

Tigger had been listening nearby. He bounced up to Rabbit and knocked him into the snow. "Come on, Rabbit," Tigger cried. "Let's bounce together!"

A Different Kind of Friendship

from *The Fox and the Hound*

A true friend stays true through good times and bad.

ne day, a young fox and a young hound met in the woods. Neither knew that foxes and hounds were not supposed to get on with each other.

"I'm a fox," said one. "My name's Tod. What's your name?"

"Mine's Copper. I'm a hound dog!"

"Gee," said Tod. "I bet you'd be good at playing hide-and-seek. Want to try it, Copper?"

All afternoon the fox and hound played together. Before they headed home, Tod said, "You're my best friend, Copper."

"And you're mine, too, Tod."

Copper grinned. "And we'll always be friends, forever. Won't we?"

"Yeah, forever!" replied Tod.

Copper lived with an old dog called Chief and a hunter named Amos Slade. Tod lived with Widow Tweed, a kind-hearted woman who took him in after he had lost his mother.

As the months passed, Amos took Copper into the woods and taught him how to hunt. Widow Tweed kept Tod at home, where he would be safe from Amos and other hunters.

One night, Tod sneaked out to visit Copper.

"You have to go, Tod!" said Copper. "'I'm a hunting dog now. And you'd better get out of here before Chief wakes up."

Chief heard them. He chased Tod onto a railway line. A train sped toward them, and Tod flattened himself between the rails. Chief was knocked off the tracks into a ravine below. He survived, but was injured.

Tod crept home to Widow Tweed's.

Widow Tweed learned about the accident from Amos. The very next day, Widow Tweed took Tod to a wildlife refuge.

Amos was still angry at Tod for having caused Chief's injuries. With Copper beside him, Amos went to the wildlife refuge to catch the young fox.

When Amos and Copper saw Tod, they pursued him through the woods. Tod could not believe that his friend Copper was chasing him.

As Tod dashed through the undergrowth, a huge bear lumbered out of the woods and swiped at Amos and Copper.

Tod turned and saw the bear towering over his old friend. He leaped onto the bear's back and bit him, then lured the bear to the river and onto a fallen log. The log snapped, and both animals tumbled into the water. While the bear lay unconscious, Tod swam to the riverbank.

Amos stood on the bank with a gun. As the hunter took aim, Copper jumped in front of Tod. The fox had just saved their lives!

Amos thought for a moment, then lowered the gun.

Soon after, Copper and Tod said goodbye to each other. They were adults now, and their lives had changed. Yet in their hearts they would remain friends forever.

Oliver on His Own

from *Oliver & Company*

When good luck comes your way, a friend is happy for you.

 ne day a ginger kitten was left on a street corner, hungry and alone. He tried to steal sausages from a vendor with the help of a stray dog named Dodger, but Dodger snatched the sausages and ran away.

The kitten followed Dodger to an abandoned barge. There he met some other dogs and their master, a good-hearted thief named Fagin.

He seemed happy to see the kitten. He scratched him under his chin and said, "We've never had a kitten in our gang before. We need all the help we can get!"

The kitten wondered if he had finally found a home, but he wasn't quite sure what kind of life he would have with Fagin and the gang. Fagin owed a great deal of money to Sykes, a vicious man with two Doberman pinschers.

The next day, Fagin sent the gang out to find some loot. As the kitten and Tito, a fast-talking Chihuahua, tried to take a stereo from a limousine, the kitten got trapped in the car with a little girl, Jenny. She seemed as lonely as the kitten. Her parents were away on a trip, and she had just learned that they wouldn't be home in time for her birthday.

Jenny hugged the kitten and said, "Poor little kitty. I'm going to take you home."

Jenny fed the kitten and gave him a warm bed to sleep in. She also gave him a name: Oliver. Jenny took Oliver to a jewellery shop and had a gold tag engraved with his name and address on it.

Just as Oliver was getting used to his new life, Fagin's gang grabbed him and took him back to the barge.

"I was happy there," Oliver moaned. "Why did you guys take me?"

"What do you mean, kid?" asked Dodger. "You're part of our gang. Hey, this place not good enough for you any more?" he said, sounding hurt.

Oliver struggled to explain. "No, I like everyone in the gang. But there was a little girl, and . . . Dodger, I just want to go back!"

Just then Fagin saw the gold tag around Oliver's neck. He assumed that Oliver's owner was terribly rich, so he wrote a ransom note. But when Jenny appeared with her piggy bank, Fagin didn't have the heart to take it from her.

As Fagin was handing Oliver over to Jenny, Sykes pulled up in his big car and grabbed the little girl. He would demand a ransom from her parents!

After a wild chase, Fagin and the gang rescued Jenny. The little girl was so grateful that she invited the whole gang over to her house to celebrate her birthday. Afterwards, Oliver followed Dodger outside.

"Thanks for everything, Dodger."

Dodger replied, "Take care of yourself, kid. And if you ever need anything, you'll know where to find me."

The Guest of Honour

from *Beauty and the Beast*

When guests come, let everything you do say, "Welcome!"

Belle was locked away in the Beast's castle, lonely and frightened. She had agreed to stay at the castle so that her father could be free. Now she was alone and feeling very sad.

Quietly she peeked out of her door. The Beast was nowhere in sight. Holding her breath, Belle tiptoed along the long hallway and down the curved staircase. A light shone from the kitchen.

Belle decided things couldn't get much worse, so she bravely pushed the door of the kitchen open.

"Good evening, mademoiselle!" cried Lumiere, the candlestick. He rushed forward to take Belle's hand. Then he bowed deeply and kissed it.

"Well, look who's here!" declared Mrs Potts cheerfully. "What can we get for you, love?"

Belle began to feel a little better. They might be household objects, but their smiles were bright and they seemed anxious to make her feel at home.

"Well, I am a little hungry," Belle admitted.

That was all they needed to hear. Suddenly the room was alive with activity as forks and spoons leaped from the drawers, and dishes and glasses rolled from the cabinets. Belle found herself being led into the dining room as tantalizing dishes danced past her: breads, stews, vegetables, meats. And the desserts – pies and cakes and puddings and pastries! Fruits and drinks of every kind presented themselves. Belle began to clap in the excitement of it all.

Mrs Potts bustled about, happy to show off her skills. Cogsworth felt very important directing all the dishes and foods in Belle's direction. And charming Lumiere made sure Belle's every wish was granted.

The grand show went on and on. Everyone wanted to do something to welcome their guest. Belle was dazzled by all the trouble

everyone went to to make sure she was happy. The room rocked with the singing and dancing of every pot, pan and plate in the castle. Even the napkins swirled like ballerinas.

At last Belle's meal was finished. "Bravo!" she exclaimed, jumping from her seat to applaud.

Lumiere, Cogsworth and Mrs Potts smiled modestly. "Oh, it was nothing," they said.

But it was something very special indeed. Belle knew that her new friends had risked the Beast's anger just to make her feel welcome. For the first time, Belle began to have hope that maybe things would work out all right, after all!

The Greatest Sacrifice

from *Hercules*

Love never gives up.

During his stay in Thebes, Hercules had fallen in love with a young woman named Megara. He had trusted her completely, until he found out that Meg was in league with Hades, the ruler of the Underworld.

"It's not like you think!" Meg pleaded with Hercules. "I mean, I couldn't . . ." She stifled a sob. "I . . . I'm so sorry."

Hercules did not want to listen. He was so heartbroken he could hardly move. And to think, he had given up his incredible godlike strength to save Meg from Hades!

Taking advantage of Hercules' weakness, Hades set Thebes on fire and sent a one-eyed monster to destroy the hero. But Hercules didn't even bother to fight back. He let the city burn and allowed the Cyclops to pummel him.

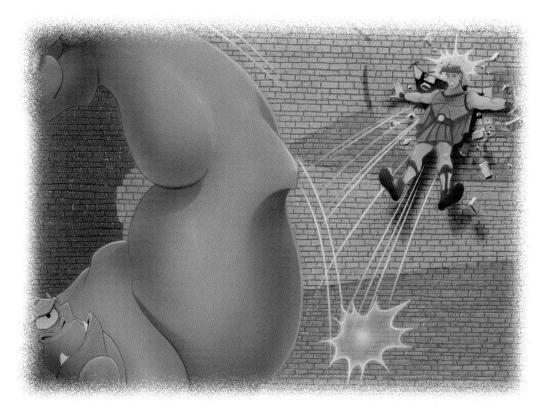

Meg hurried up to him. "Without your strength," she cried, "you'll be killed!"

"There are worse things," replied Hercules in a flat, resigned voice.

Meg could not stand by and watch Hercules be killed. She leaped onto the back of Hercules' flying horse, Pegasus, and told him to find Philoctetes, Hercules' former trainer.

They found Phil at the docks. "Herc needs your help!" Meg cried.

Phil wouldn't even look at her. "Why does he need me when he has friends like *you*?" he spat.

"He won't listen to me!" Meg replied.

"Good! He's finally learned something."

Meg wailed, "If you don't help him, Phil, he'll die!"

Phil agreed to help. With Meg, he arrived just in time to see the Cyclops dash Hercules against a pillar. "Come on, kid, fight back!" Phil cried.

Herc glanced at Meg, then focused a swollen eye on the trainer. "You were right all along, Phil. Dreams are for rookies."

"No, kid. Giving up is for rookies. I'm not quittin'. How about you?"

Hercules considered Phil's words. Then he jumped up, grabbed a burning stick, and thrust it at the monster's eye. As the Cyclops

thrashed about, howling, Hercules hastily tied a rope around the giant's ankles. The Cyclops tripped on the rope and knocked against two marble columns. As the columns wobbled, the monster plunged into the sea.

One of the pillars fell towards Hercules. "Look out!" Meg cried. She ran to Hercules and pushed him out of the way, only to have the column crash down on her.

"Meg!" Hercules pushed against the column, sweating and straining. Suddenly his godlike strength returned, and Hercules lifted up the column without any effort.

He bent down and cradled Meg in his strong arms.

"You . . . " he said, catching his breath. "You saved me. But why?"

"I guess people do crazy things when they're in love."

"Love? Oh, Meg . . . Meg . . . I, I . . ."

"Are you always this articulate?" Meg grinned weakly at him. "You can still stop Hades, but there isn't much time."

Baloo Lends a Paw

from *The Jungle Book*

Everyone needs help sometimes, and friends are eager to give it.

aloo the bear loved Mowgli more than any other animal in the jungle. He taught Mowgli all about the bare necessities of life. Sometimes he even forgot that Mowgli was really a mancub, and not a bear at all. So when Bagheera, the panther, reminded Baloo that Mowgli's place was in the village with the other men, Baloo felt very sad.

But Baloo knew that Bagheera was right. The cunning tiger, Shere Khan, was just waiting for his chance to pounce on the boy. The

sooner Mowgli was safely among his own kind, the better. But when Baloo tried to explain this to Mowgli, the boy got very angry.

"I'm not a man, I'm a bear, like you," he told Baloo.

Baloo scratched his head. He just wasn't very good at explaining things. "Now look, Mowgli. You've got to go back and that's all there is to it."

Mowgli stamped his foot. "I'm not going!" he shouted, and he dashed into the jungle.

Baloo ran after him, but the heavy bear was far too slow to catch up with the little boy. Mowgli was gone.

Mowgli roamed the jungle on his own. He didn't care what anyone said. The mancub was sure he could take care of himself just fine.

Suddenly a pair of hypnotic eyes entranced him. Kaa, the snake, had caught Mowgli in his coils! He was all set to make a meal out of the boy when a cold voice interrupted him.

"Give the mancub to me, Kaa!" snarled Shere Khan.

"Not so fast, Shere Khan!" shouted a familiar voice. It was Baloo!

"Get this kid out of here," Baloo ordered. A group of vultures swooped down and carried Mowgli to safety.

Mowgli watched as Baloo fought with Shere Khan. Even the vultures were hoping Baloo would win. Baloo fought bravely for his little friend, but the tiger seemed to be winning.

A bolt of lightning struck a nearby tree. "Fire!" shouted the vultures. "Shere Khan is afraid of it!"

Mowgli quickly grabbed a burning branch and tied it to the tiger's tail. Shere Khan howled as the flames burned his fur, and raced away, never to be seen again.

Mowgli sighed in relief. He was safe, thanks to the vultures and his loyal friend, Baloo the bear.

Stick Together

from *Toy Story*

Friendship can take you to infinity and beyond.

Woody the cowboy stood up tall in his cowboy boots, waving his arms to make the other toys notice him.

"Attention! Attention everyone!" he shouted. The noisy toys lined up in front of him. They were all very nervous and excited. Today was moving day!

"All right, now that everyone is here, let's get started," Woody said. "We have to stick together to make sure no one gets left behind in the move. So we each have to pick a moving partner."

"Howdy, pardner," joked a rubber chicken.

"It's not funny," said Woody. "Now, I'll pick . . . Bo Peep."

Nobody was surprised. Woody and Bo were sweethearts.

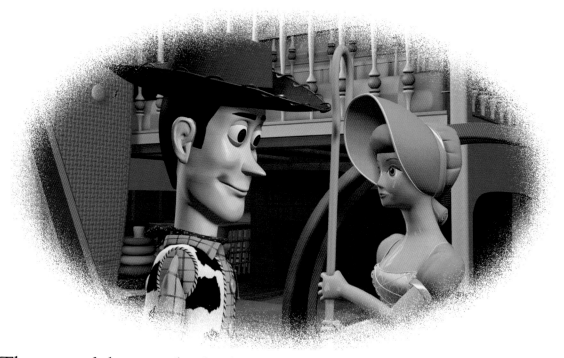

The rest of the toys had a harder time choosing partners. Rex the dinosaur was so worried about being left behind, he chose 100 moving buddies! All of them were little green soldiers. Rex felt safer with them.

All the toys started arguing about who would be pairing up.

"Everybody calm down," Woody shouted over the din. But just then, Andy burst through the door. All the toys froze where they were.

Andy began tossing toys into a box. Downstairs, his mother called to him to hurry up.

Woody glanced under the bed. A teddy bear waved back. As soon as Andy's back was turned, Woody pushed the bear into the light.

"Mum, I found Molly's bear!" Andy yelled, tossing it into the box. He was searching through the toys. "Hey, Mum! I can't find Buzz!" Andy shouted.

The toys looked at one another. Buzz Lightyear, the spaceman, was one of Andy's favourite toys. They all thought he had been packed already!

Woody was beginning to panic. He couldn't just leave his friend behind! Suddenly, the answer came to him. Andy always took a toy with him when he delivered newspapers on his bicycle. Buzz must be in the bike basket!

Soon all the toys were packed and loaded into the car. Woody peeked out of the box. Andy's bike was strapped to the back of the car, but there was no sign of Buzz. Woody told Bo he had to switch partners. Carefully, he climbed out of the car and slid into the bike basket.

"Howdy, moving partner!" he told a surprised Buzz Lightyear. "Permission to come aboard?"

Together, the friends rode to their new home.

A Lovely Bella Notte

from *Lady and the Tramp*

Every night is beautiful when you're with the one you love.

ady, a pretty cocker spaniel from the nice side of town, was a bit nervous. She was not at all sure if she should trust Tramp. But the stray had saved her life.

"Hey!" Tramp cried, struck by a great idea. "Let's go to Tony's! The perfect place for a special occasion. Come on."

Lady followed Tramp to a restaurant that glowed with candlelight. Delicious smells wafted out, and Lady could hear someone singing. Entranced, she started towards the front door.

"No!" Tramp whispered. "This way. I have my own private entrance."

He turned down a dark alley.

Lady hesitated. The alley looked scary. But she couldn't back out now.

"Wait here," Tramp instructed.

Lady hid behind a rubbish bin and watched Tramp scratch on the restaurant's back door.

A moment later, a big, friendly-looking man wearing an apron opened the door.

"Hello, Butch!" he said. "Where have you been, huh?"

The man seemed very happy to see him. Tramp licked his face.

"Hey, Joe," the man yelled into the restaurant. "Bring some bones for Butch before he eats me up."

"Okay, Tony," Joe called. "Some bones coming right up."

Tramp seemed a little disappointed. The truth was, he was hoping for more elegant fare.

He ran over to Lady and barked loudly.

"What's this?" Tony asked. Then he saw Lady and smiled.

"Hey, Joe," Tony shouted. "Butch has a new girlfriend."

Tony scratched Lady under the jaw and all her nervousness disappeared.

He went back into the restaurant, and in a moment returned with a small table covered with a red-and-white checked tablecloth. He put down breadsticks and a candle.

For us? Lady marvelled. She had never been allowed to dine at the table before.

The couple sat down. Tramp studied the menu thoughtfully and then barked their order.

"Hey, Joe," Tony shouted. "Butch would like the spaghetti special, heavy on the meatballs."

Lady was impressed.

In a few minutes, Tony placed a large plate heaped with spaghetti and meatballs before them. It smelt delicious!

Lady took a dainty bite. It tasted as good as it smelt.

As the lovely cocker spaniel was thinking about what an exciting and wonderful evening she was having, Tony and Joe began singing an Italian song about a beautiful night.

This beautiful night, Lady thought, and looked into Tramp's friendly brown eyes.

The Perfect Presents for Eeyore

from *Winnie the Pooh and a Day for Eeyore*

⬦⬦⬦

The best thing about any present is that someone thought to give it to you.

Pooh was hurrying home after seeing Eeyore. Pooh felt awful. It was Eeyore's birthday, and nobody had remembered to get him a present.

Outside his house he found Piglet. "I have just seen poor Eeyore," he panted, "and he is very sad, because it's his birthday, and nobody has taken any notice of it."

They went inside. Pooh went straight to his cupboard to fetch a small jar of honey.

"I'm giving this to Eeyore as a present. What are *you* going to give?"

Piglet thought for a moment. "I know. I'll give him a balloon. I'll go and get it now!"

So off Piglet trotted, and in the other direction went Pooh.

Pooh hadn't gone far when a funny feeling began to creep all over him. It was just as if somebody inside him were saying, "Now then, Pooh, time for a little snack."

So he sat down and began to eat from his jar of honey.

Now let me see, he thought, as he took his last lick of honey. Where was I going?

And then, suddenly, he remembered. He had eaten Eeyore's birthday present!

"*Bother!*" said Pooh. "What shall I do?"

For a little while he couldn't think of anything. Then he thought, Well, it's a very nice pot, even if there's no honey in it, and if I washed it clean, and got Owl to write "A Happy Birthday" on it, Eeyore could keep things in it which might be useful.

So he went to call on Owl.

"Good morning, Owl," he said.

"Good morning, Pooh," said Owl.

"It's Eeyore's birthday," said Pooh. "I'm giving him a useful pot to keep things in, and I wanted to ask you–"

"You ought to write 'A Happy Birthday' on it."

"That's what I wanted to ask you," said Pooh. "Would you write it for me?"

So Owl wrote:

HIPY PAPY BTHUTHDTH THU HDA BTHUTHDY.

"It's nice and long," said Pooh, very much impressed.

"Well, actually," said Owl, "it says 'A Very Happy Birthday with Love from Pooh.'"

"Oh, I see," said Pooh.

In the meantime, Piglet had gone home to get the balloon. He held it very tightly against himself, so that it shouldn't blow away, and he ran to Eeyore as fast as he could. And running along, thinking how pleased Eeyore would be, he didn't look where he was going . . . and fell down flat on his face.

BANG!!!!

It was the balloon.

"Oh, dear!" said Piglet. "Well, it's too late now. I don't have another balloon."

So he trotted on, rather sadly now, and came to the side of the stream where Eeyore was.

"Good morning, Eeyore," he called.

"Good morning, Piglet," said Eeyore.

"Many happy returns of the day," said Piglet.

"Meaning me?" Eeyore turned to stare at Piglet. "My birthday?"

"Of course, Eeyore," Piglet said. "And I've brought you a present. A balloon."

"Balloon?" said Eeyore. "One of those big coloured things you blow up?"

"Yes," said Piglet, "but I'm afraid . . . I'm very sorry, Eeyore, but when I was running along to bring it to you, I fell and I burst the balloon."

"My balloon?" said Eeyore at last. "My birthday balloon?"

"Yes, Eeyore," said Piglet. "Here it is. With many happy returns of the day."

"Thank you, Piglet," said Eeyore. "Hmm. It was a red balloon," Eeyore murmured to himself.

Piglet was trying to think of something to say when he heard a shout from the other side of the river. It was Pooh.

"I've brought you a little present," said Pooh excitedly. "Here it is. It's a useful pot. And it's got 'A Very Happy Birthday with Love from Pooh' written on it. And it's for putting things in!"

When Eeyore saw the pot, he became quite excited. "Look, Piglet!" said Eeyore. "I believe my balloon will just go into that pot!"

"I'm very glad," said Pooh happily, "that I thought of giving you a useful pot to put things in."

"I'm very glad," said Piglet happily, "that I thought of giving you something to put in a useful pot."

But Eeyore wasn't listening. He was taking the balloon out, and putting it back in again, as happy as could be.

A Royal Pet

from *Aladdin*

⁓⁓⁓

Some of the most loyal friends have whiskers.

Prince Achmed, one of Princess Jasmine's many suitors, stumbled out of the palace. His pride had been wounded, his vanity stung, and the seat of his trousers ripped off.

Jasmine thought him the worst suitor of the lot. Ugly. Arrogant. And he had a snakelike, curling moustache that reminded her of her father's cruel advisor, Jafar.

Now she sat by the fountain, thinking. As always, her pet tiger, Rajah, was by her side.

Suddenly Jasmine's sad thoughts were interrupted.

"Jasmine! Jasmine!" It was the Sultan, her father.

Rajah growled right in the Sultan's face, clutching a piece of Prince Achmed's underpants in his teeth.

"So *this* is why Prince Achmed stormed out!" the Sultan cried.

"Oh, Father," Jasmine teased. "Rajah was just playing with him. Weren't you, Rajah?"

"Dearest," the Sultan scolded, "you've got to stop rejecting every suitor who comes to call. The law says you must be married to a prince by your next birthday."

Jasmine sighed. "The law is wrong," she declared, though she knew her father wasn't listening.

She hugged Rajah close. Even if her father didn't understand, Rajah did. He loved her and knew the secrets of her heart. Her pet would do anything to help her. Jasmine realized how lucky she was to have a friend like Rajah.

A Lagoon Tune

from *The Little Mermaid*

—⊶⊷—

Your eyes give voice to the love in your heart.

It had been such a romantic day for Ariel. Prince Eric had taken her all over his kingdom in his carriage. Ariel loved seeing all the things she had only dreamed of before, living under the sea, but the best part was spending time with Eric.

The only problem was, she couldn't tell him how she felt. Ursula the Sea Witch had taken her voice in payment for changing her into a human being. Ariel longed to know if Eric felt the same way about her, but all she could do was wait and hope that he would say he loved her.

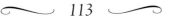

Eric knew that he was falling in love with the young woman he had rescued from the beach, but it was so hard to tell how she felt. He wished there were some way to know what was on her mind.

That evening, Eric took Ariel for a romantic boat ride. Fireflies glowed all around them. Ariel smiled hopefully at Eric.

"I wish I knew your name," Eric told her.

"Her name is Ariel," whispered Sebastian, Ariel's friend.

"Ariel?" Eric guessed. "That's pretty."

Ariel smiled. Things were going in the right direction.

"So, when's he going to pucker up?" Scuttle the seagull asked Sebastian. Ariel's friends were getting impatient. They knew that if Eric didn't fall in love with Ariel by sunset the next day, Ariel would have to return to Ursula and become her prisoner.

"This boy needs some help," Sebastian decided. He grabbed a reed and held it up like a baton.

The frogs and birds and fish gathered around as Sebastian led them in a romantic love song.

"Go on – kiss the girl," they urged Eric.

Ariel fluttered her eyelashes at Eric. Did he feel the same way about her as she did about him?

The tiny rowing boat drifted in the moonlight. It was a magical night. Eric looked at Ariel and knew he was in love with her.

"Kiss the girl!" Sebastian repeated in Eric's ear.

Eric and Ariel leant towards each other. They were about to kiss when . . .

SPLASH!

Flotsam and Jetsam, Ursula's pet eels, tipped the boat over and dumped Ariel and Eric into the cold water. The moment was ruined.

Ariel sighed as Eric helped her up. Eric had come so close to kissing her! But she knew there would be another chance, because even with no words spoken, she was sure he loved her, too.

Missing: Christopher Robin

from *Pooh's Grand Adventure: The Search for Christopher Robin*

Good friends look out for each other.

Ever since Winnie the Pooh could remember (which wasn't much further back than yesterday), he could count on meeting Christopher Robin at their favourite place in the Hundred-Acre Wood – a lovely, enchanted hill.

But one day, instead of finding Chrisopher Robin, Pooh found a pot of honey and a note instead.

Later, Owl read the note to Pooh and his friends. "Christopher Robin," Owl declared, "has gone to Skull!"

"Skull?!" Tigger cried. "Are you absoposilutely sure an' certain?"

Owl snorted. "What else can S-C-H-O-O-L spell?"

"You got me there, featherhead," replied Tigger. "Sure sounds terrifryin', don't it?"

Owl and Eeyore and Rabbit and Piglet agreed, and most of all Pooh, who was afraid for his friend. "We must get Christopher Robin back!" Pooh exclaimed.

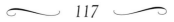

"Good luck!" said Owl, who had decided not to join the rescue expedition. "Toodle-oo! I'll keep a sharp eye out for your return . . . if you do return, of course."

Owl's farewell made the friends nervous, but not as much as Tigger's talk of the horrible Skullasaurus they were sure to meet at Skull.

Still, the friends trekked on. They picked their way through the Forest of Thorns. They roamed through the Valley of Flowers. They wobbled across the bridge that spanned the Screaming Gorge, and they wandered through the Valley of Mists. After much tramping and tromping, they arrived at Skull Cave.

If they were going to save Christopher Robin, they knew they must venture inside. The friends tiptoed into the deep, dark cave. Inside, something GRRROWLED!

"The Skullasaurus!" cried Piglet. He ran in one direction. Pooh ran in another. Eeyore ran one way. Tigger ran the other.

The friends bumped into one another in the Crystal Cavern. And something found them. It was a shadow. And it GRRROWLED!

The shadow moved towards them. It was Christopher Robin!

"Where have you been?" cried the boy. "I've been searching everywhere for you!"

"We've been searching for you!" Piglet cried. "We wanted to save you from Skull!"

"Skull?" said Christopher Robin, smiling. "I was at school."

"But what about the Skullasaurus?" asked Piglet. "We heard him!"

Christopher Robin gently pointed out that the growl was the rumbly tumbly of a hungry-for-honey Pooh Bear.

Then everyone, including Christopher Robin, tramped home for a feast of their favourite foods: haycorn pie for Piglet and Rabbit, thistles for Eeyore, malt extract for Tigger, and honey, of course, for Pooh.

SAVING THE DAY

STORIES ABOUT COURAGE AND RESPONSIBILITY

Born to Be King

from *The Lion King*

❦

You can't change the past, but you can improve the future.

One day, Nala, an old friend of Simba, appeared in the jungle and begged Simba to return to Pride Rock, where Scar, Simba's wicked uncle, had assumed the place of king.

"I can't go back," Simba insisted. "Look, sometimes bad things happen, and there's nothing you can do about it. So why worry?"

Simba told Nala he couldn't help her and walked away.

That night, Simba wandered across a high grassy plain. *What would it prove if I went back to Pride Rock?* he thought. *It won't change anything. You can't change the past.*

As Simba roamed, a baboon jumped out of a tree and followed him. "Will you stop following me?" Simba growled. "Who are you?"

Rafiki said, "The question is: who are you?"

"I thought I knew." Simba sighed. "But now I'm not so sure."

Rafiki chuckled. "I know who you are. You're Mufasa's boy."

"You knew my father?" Simba asked, amazed.

"Correction!" Rafiki replied. "I *know* your father."

Simba shook his head sadly. "I hate to tell you this, but he died a long time ago."

"Nope!" the baboon chortled. "Wrong again! He's alive. I'll show him to you. You follow old Rafiki. He knows the way!"

Simba followed Rafiki to a pool. Rafiki parted the reeds and said, "Shh. Look down there."

Simba peered into the water, hoping to see a miracle. "That's not my father," he said quietly. "That's just my reflection."

"No," Rafiki insisted. "Look *harder*."

Simba tried. It was true that he looked like Mufasa, but . . .

"See?" said Rafiki. "Your father lives on in you."

Then Simba heard Mufasa's regal voice booming from the heavens. He looked up at the stars.

"Simba," commanded Mufasa, "you must take your place in the circle of life. Remember who you are. You are my son, and the one true king. Remember . . . remember . . ."

As the voice faded, Rafiki winked and said, "What was that? The weather . . . very peculiar!"

"Looks like the winds are changing," said Simba.

"Change is good!" replied Rafiki.

"Yeah," said Simba, "but it's not easy. I know what I have to do, but going back means that I'll have to face my past. I've been running from it for so long."

Rafiki lifted his cane and hit Simba on the head.

"Ow!" cried Simba. "What was that for?"

Rafiki laughed. "It doesn't matter. It's in the past!"

"Yeah," said Simba, rubbing his head, "but it still hurts."

"Oh, yes, the past can hurt, but the way I see it, you either run from it . . . or learn from it."

Simba was convinced. He ran through the tall grass, heading for Pride Rock. He *would* challenge Scar. It was time.

Mulan Saves the Day

from *Mulan*

There are many ways to fight, but the best is with your brain.

At the Tung-Shao Pass, high in the snow-covered peaks of China, the Huns attacked Captain Shang and his troops without warning. Hundreds of flaming arrows descended on Shang's men from somewhere up the mountain.

"Get out of range!" Shang cried. "Save the cannons!"

The soldiers carried the cannons back behind some rocks and aimed them at the enemy.

"Fire!" Shang shouted.

Mulan, disguised as a man, fired a cannon at the snipers above her. The rockets exploded, and the Huns fired back with more arrows. Mulan and the other soldiers ducked.

"Hold the last cannon!" Shang commanded. His troops waited, peering through the haze. The mountains were silent. As the smoke cleared, Mulan and the others gasped. On top of the ridge, along the entire horizon, stretched a massive line of Huns. In front rode Shan-Yu, the Hun leader.

In a firm, solemn voice, Shang ordered, "Prepare to fight. If we die, we die with honour."

"Hee-yah!" cried Shan-Yu, charging down the mountain with his troops.

"Yao!" Shang shouted to one of his men. "Aim the last cannon at Shan-Yu!"

Mulan stood beside Yao, her sword drawn. She looked down at her blade and saw the mountain reflected in its shiny surface. She gazed up at the mountain, then at the charging Huns.

Quickly Mulan sheathed her sword and grabbed the cannon away from Yao.

"Ping!" called Shang, using the man's name Mulan had invented to disguise herself. "Come back! Ping!"

As Shan-Yu galloped toward her, Mulan carried the cannon up the mountain. Suddenly she stopped. She placed the cannon in front of Shan-Yu, then tilted the barrel towards the top of the mountain.

Mulan fired, and the rocket sailed over Shan-Yu's head. It lodged in the overhanging mountaintop, then exploded with a thunderous roar, causing a massive avalanche.

As the wall of snow thundered towards Shan-Yu, the Hun leader glared at Mulan. He had been outwitted! And by an ordinary soldier, no less. Shan-Yu slashed at Mulan, but she hurried away, eager to escape the monstrous force rumbling down the mountain. The avalanche overtook Shan-Yu and his men, and the Huns were defeated.

Who's Afraid of the Big Bad Wolf?

from *Three Little Pigs*

Taking the easy way out usually makes things harder.

nce upon a time, three little pigs lived at the edge of a forest. They were brothers, and their names were Fifer Pig, Fiddler Pig and Practical Pig. Fifer and Fiddler loved nothing more than to sing and dance all day long. Their brother Practical was more, well, practical. Singing and dancing were fine, he thought, but one must never forget that the big bad wolf lived in the nearby woods.

When it was time for the brothers to build their homes, Fifer and Fiddler were lazy. They quickly threw together rough shacks, one made of straw, the other of sticks. They laughed as they watched their hard-working brother Practical build his own home out of sturdy bricks.

"You can't be too careful," Practical warned them. "The wolf may come someday, and then what?"

"Ha!" laughed Fifer and Fiddler. They danced jigs and played music, but Practical went on working until at last his strong house of bricks was finished.

Just as Practical had feared, the wolf soon learned of the fat little pigs living at the edge of the woods. He wasted no time in paying the brothers a visit.

"Little pig, little pig, let me come in!" the wolf barked.

"Not by the hair of my chinny-chin-chin!" squealed Fifer Pig.

"Then I'll huff and I'll puff and I'll blow your house in!" And sure enough, the wolf blew down the house of

straw. Fifer ran to Fiddler's house, and the wolf soon followed.

"Little pigs, little pigs, let me come in!"

"Not by the hairs of our chinny-chin-chins!" squealed the pigs. And so the wolf easily blew down the house of sticks as well.

Quickly the frightened pigs ran to Practical's house.

"Little pigs, little pigs, let me come in!" howled the hungry wolf.

"Not by the hairs of our chinny-chin-chins!" the pigs replied. This time the huffing and puffing did nothing to the solid house of brick.

But the wolf did not give up. The pigs heard him climbing up to the roof. So they lit a fire and boiled some water in a big pot.

Suddenly they heard the wolf slipping down the chimney. He landed with a splash in the pot of boiling water.

"YOWEEEEE!" shrieked the wolf. He leaped back up the chimney as fast as he could and ran back to the forest, never to be seen again.

But just to be on the safe side, Fifer and Fiddler built new brick houses for themselves the very next day.

Fit for a Princess

from *Cinderella*

Don't be afraid to make yourself heard.

The morning after the ball, Cinderella gazed longingly at the glass slipper, her only reminder of the wonderful time she had spent at the ball. Thanks to her fairy godmother, Cinderella had left her household chores behind and spent one perfect, magical night dancing with a handsome stranger.

When Cinderella heard her stepmother calling, she put the slipper away and hurried downstairs.

As Cinderella stood at the door, she heard her stepmother say to her stepsisters, "The Grand Duke has been hunting all night for the girl who lost her slipper at the ball. The Duke has been ordered to try the glass slipper on every girl in the kingdom, and if the one can be found whose foot fits the slipper, then that girl shall be the Prince's bride!"

Cinderella forgot all about her chores. Last night she had been dancing with the Prince! "I must get dressed," she murmured. "It would never do for the Duke to see me like this. . . ."

Having overheard her, the stepmother knew that Cinderella had been the girl at the ball. She followed Cinderella upstairs and locked her in her room.

The Grand Duke soon arrived. Anastasia was the first to try on the slipper. "I knew it was my slipper!" she said to the footman. "It's exactly my size." The slipper barely fitted over Anastasia's toes. "Oh, well," spluttered Anastasia, "it may be a trifle snug today. You know how it is, dancing all night . . . it's always fit before!"

The Grand Duke sniffed, not believing a word, and asked Drizella to try on the slipper. "Get away from me," she snapped at the footman. "I'll make it fit!"

But nothing Drizella did could make the slipper fit.

As the Grand Duke prepared to leave, Cinderella flew down the stairs. Her friends, the mice, had stolen the key to her room from her stepmother's pocket and freed her.

"May I try on the slipper?" Cinderella cried out. As the footman approached, the stepmother stuck out her cane and tripped him. The glass slipper crashed to the floor and shattered.

The Grand Duke exclaimed, "This is terrible! What will the King say? What will he do?"

Cinderella said, "But perhaps I can help . . ."

"Nothing can help now," moaned the Grand Duke, his head in his hands.

"But you see," said Cinderella, reaching into her pocket, "I have the other slipper."

The Grand Duke placed the glass slipper on Cinderella's foot. To his delight, it fitted perfectly!

And so Cinderella was taken to the palace, where she and the Prince lived happily ever after.

Silly Old Bear

from *Winnie the Pooh and the Honey Tree*

Before you act, you need to think, think, think.

Pooh was feeling a bit rumbly in his tumbly, as Pooh Bears often do.

"Time for a smackerel of something sweet," Pooh decided. Just then, a buzzing honeybee zipped under Pooh's nose. "Aha!" cried Pooh, following the bee. Pooh knew that bees made honey, and wherever the bee went, there was sure to be some. The bee flew into a hive high above Pooh's head.

All Pooh could think about was getting his paws on the honey in that hive. But how? He decided to get Christopher Robin's help.

"Ah, Christopher Robin, I was wondering if you, ah, if you had a balloon?" he asked his friend innocently. "For getting honey, you see."

Christopher Robin gently told Pooh that one doesn't get honey with balloons. However, Pooh had a plan to fool the bees, and the balloon was an important part of it.

Christopher Robin watched as Pooh rolled in some mud until he was covered completely. "What are you supposed to be?" he asked.

"I'm a little black rain cloud, of course," Pooh told him. Then he held tight to the balloon and rose up, up, up to the hive.

Pooh called down to Christopher Robin. "It might help if you picked up your umbrella and said, 'Tut, tut, it looks like rain.'"

"Silly old bear!" Christopher Robin laughed. Pooh's plans never quite worked out the way he hoped. But Christopher Robin did as his friend asked.

The bees were suspicious. They had never seen a rain cloud like this one before! And when Pooh greedily scooped their honey into his mouth, they went into action!

ZOOM! flew the bees, 100 at a time. Pooh held tight to his balloon as the bees swarmed around him. Buzzzzz, buzzzz, buzzzz!

Pooh realized that his plan wasn't working. "I think these may be the wrong sort of bees," he said to himself.

The bees kept coming at Pooh. Buzzz, buzzz, buzzz!

"Christopher Robin!" shouted Pooh. "Help!"

The bees crowded around Pooh and his balloon. Suddenly the balloon popped and began to streak through the air. Pooh held on until it was empty. Then he began to fall to the ground with the bees close behind.

"Over here, Pooh!" called Christopher Robin. Christopher Robin and Pooh jumped into the mud puddle as the bees flew past.

"Christopher Robin, you never can tell with bees," mused Pooh.

Jafar's Just Desserts

from *Aladdin*

⌘

Brains beat strength every time.

Jafar was determined to destroy Aladdin, Jasmine and the Sultan once and for all. With a mighty roar, he unleashed all his power. The palace crumbled and the earth cracked. Jafar cackled with evil glee. He knew that even the Genie was no match for him in strength.

But the Genie had a trick up his sleeve. He had disguised himself as Aladdin.

"Give it up, Jafar!" the Genie shouted. His stance was bold, though he looked tiny and weak next to the monstrous Jafar. "I'm obviously too much for you to handle!"

"You!" Jafar snarled, enraged beyond rage. His deep voice rumbled and boomed. "You are a fool to challenge me. I am all powerful!"

The Genie taunted him fearlessly in Aladdin's voice. "So all powerful you can't even get rid of a lowly street rat?"

"A problem I mean to rectify right now!" Jafar shouted. Quickly he changed into a huge snake. There was some truth in the Genie's words, but now was his chance to squeeze the life out of Aladdin once and for all!

Jafar grabbed the Genie in one huge red coil. But as Jafar began to squeeze, Aladdin changed right before Jafar's eyes – into the Genie!

"What?!" Jafar gasped.

"Gotcha!" The Genie smiled. He zapped the serpent into a genie – a powerful enemy, but one who would be trapped forever in a magic lamp.

As Jafar disappeared into the lamp, the Genie laughed. "You may be stronger, Jafar, but I've got the brains!"

It's a Good Life!

from *Snow White and the Seven Dwarfs*

When you've worked your hardest you can feel your proudest.

nce upon a time, deep in the woods, there lived seven dwarfs: Doc, Dopey, Sleepy, Bashful, Sneezy, Happy and Grumpy. Their names were all perfectly suited to their personalities.

Since dwarfs are as small as children, their cosy cottage was like a doll's house. It had a thick wooden door framed by leafy vines. And inside, everything was the perfect size for them.

Despite their different personalities, the dwarfs got along quite

Despite their different personalities, the dwarfs got along quite
well. From sunrise to sunset, they shared the same goal – to do a good
job and reap the fruits of their labour.

Every day, after a hearty breakfast of porridge and freshly baked
bread, the Seven Dwarfs would pick up their picks, axes and shovels
and march off to work in the mines.

As they walked, they sang cheerfully. The dwarfs always looked
forward to their day. For though their work was hard, it was rewarding.

Dwarfs have an uncanny ability for finding precious metals and stones, and they love fashioning them into beautiful things like necklaces, rings, swords and crowns.

The dwarfs' jewel mine was in the rocky hills not far from their home, and it was deep and dark. But the dwarfs were used to working underground, and they were not afraid.

Every day, as they swung their picks, chipping away at pieces of rock, they sang a work song. Their low, melodious voices echoed throughout the caverns and tunnels of the mine.

Then, at the end of each day, a clock struck five. One of the dwarfs would look up and cry, "Heigh-ho!"

In a wink, they would all collect their tools and march out of the mine in single file, in the same way as they had come.

Tired yet satisfied, each evening the dwarfs marched down the well-travelled path, whistling and singing. They were content to be heading to their pleasant home after a good day's work, and they always looked forward to the delicious stew that bubbled on the hearth.

Wilbur Takes Wing

from *The Rescuers Down Under*

Some causes are worth fighting for.

Bianca and Bernard rushed across the city rooftops, fighting to see through the blinding snow. They finally came to a big birdhouse with a sign that read ALBATROSS AIR.

Bernard peered through the frosty window. "Thank heavens!" he gasped. "The light's on!"

They pushed open the door and dropped their heavy luggage on the floor.

An albatross was dancing around the room, so absorbed in the music that he didn't even notice his tiny customers.

Bianca tapped on his foot. "Excuse us for interrupting," she said. "I'm Miss Bianca, and this is Mr Bernard. We're from the Rescue Aid Society. We need to charter a flight to Australia."

The albatross bowed and introduced himself. "The name's Wilbur. At your service. Now, when do you want to go? Mid June would be nice."

"Now," said Bianca. "Tonight."

"What??" squawked Wilbur. "Are you kidding? Have you taken a look outside lately? Sorry, no go."

"But a little boy has been kidnapped," Bernard pleaded. "We need your help."

"K-k-k-kidnapped?" Wilbur spluttered. He was shocked. Then he was angry.

"Nobody's gonna take a little kid's freedom away while I'm around. Okay, storm or no storm, let's go! Just gimme a second to loosen up the ol' back!"

With Bianca and Bernard safely strapped into a sardine tin on Wilbur's back, the albatross took off on a great adventure.

What It Takes to Be a Hero

from *Hercules*

A hero's strongest muscle is his heart.

ercules had helped drive Hades away from Mount Olympus, but his battle with the powerful ruler of the Underworld wasn't over yet.

"Gotta go collect my consolation prize," Hades sneered. "A friend of yours. I know she's *dying* to see me."

Hercules turned to watch Hades take off in his chariot. Then he realized what Hades meant. "Meg!" he cried.

Hercules leaped onto Pegasus' back and raced toward Thebes, praying he would reach Meg in time.

But he was too late. Hades had already taken Meg's soul.

"Meg! No!" He cried.

Hercules carefully lifted Meg in his arms. Her body was cold
and lifeless.

"Sorry, kid," said Phil, wiping a tear from his eye. "Some things you
just can't change."

"Oh, yes, I can," Hercules vowed. "Yes, I can!"

He rode Pegasus down to the Underworld and confronted Hades.

"Where's Meg?" he demanded.

Hades couldn't believe his eyes. "Wonder Boy," he said, "you're too
much. You know no one visits here . . . by choice."

"Let her go!" demanded Hercules.

Through an archway, Hercules could see a whirlpool filled with a swirling mass of souls. He caught sight of Meg for a moment. She was heading towards the pit of death.

"Meg!" he cried. He plunged his arms into the pool but pulled back in horror. His hands and arms had begun to age!

"No, no! Mustn't touch," laughed Hades.

Hercules tried to think quickly. He had to do something to save Meg. There had to be some way to reverse her fate.

Suddenly he knew what to do. "You like making deals," Hercules said. "Take me in Meg's place."

"Hmm," said Hades, considering the offer. "The son of my hated rival trapped forever in the river of death?"

"Going once," said Hercules.

"Is there a downside to this?"

"Going twice . . ."

"Okay, okay," Hades agreed. "It's a deal. You fish Meg out. She goes, you stay."

Hercules took a deep breath and dived into the vortex of souls. Instantly he could feel his body beginning to age. But he struggled on towards Meg. By the time he reached her, he was almost a skeleton. Still, he managed to grab hold of her.

Suddenly he felt something happening to him. His whole body was being filled with a strength and light beyond his wildest dreams. He carried Meg's soul out of the pit.

Hades looked on, horrified. "You can't be alive," he stammered. "You'd have to be . . ."

"A god?" finished Pain and Panic.

And it was true. Hercules' godhood had been restored.

He guided Meg's spirit to her lifeless body. And before his eyes, she came back to life. He took her in his arms and held her tight.

As they embraced, bolts of lightning struck the ground at their feet. They rose heavenward on a cloud until they came to an enormous stairway – the stairway that led to the gates of Mount Olympus, home of the gods.

As the pair started up the stairs, all the gods gave Hercules a standing ovation. Risking everything to save Meg, he had finally proven himself a true hero.

Mulan's Test

from *Mulan*

Solving a problem requires both determination and inspiration.

"I don't need anyone causing trouble in my camp." The captain, Shang, was looking right at Mulan, and she was mortified. Disguised as a man, she had just arrived at the army training camp – and she was already making mistakes! Because of her, a huge cauldron of rice had been knocked over and there was rice everywhere.

"Thanks to your friend Ping," Shang continued, pointing to Mulan, "you will spend tonight picking up every single grain of rice.

And tomorrow, the real work begins!" The other soldiers glared accusingly at her. She groaned inwardly.

The next morning, Mulan was awakened by her friend Mushu the dragon. "All right. Rise and shine, sleeping beauty!"

Mulan was exhausted from staying up the whole night before, and every muscle in her body ached. Pulling her clothes on as fast as she could, she rushed to catch up with the rest of the men.

Shang was already addressing the troops. "You will assemble swiftly and silently. And anyone who acts otherwise will answer to me." He pulled an arrow out and drew his bow. The men in the front row jumped back, terrified. Shang fired the arrow at a high wooden pole behind him.

He motioned to Yao, one of the soldiers who had been taunting Mulan earlier. "Thanks for volunteering. Retrieve that arrow."

"Oh, I'll get that arrow, pretty boy." The disgruntled soldier sneered at him.

"You seem to be missing something," said Shang calmly. From a box, he removed two heavy bronze discs and tied them to Yao's wrists.

"One represents discipline. The other represents strength. You need both to reach the arrow."

Confident, Yao approached the pole. But as he tried to climb it, it became obvious that the weights were too much for him, and he crashed to the ground. Ling and Mulan also put all their effort into climbing the pole, but they both collapsed at the bottom, drained.

Disgusted with this pathetic lot of soldiers, Shang decided to begin the rest of the training. Mulan tried to practise with the others, but they were only interested in tricking her into looking bad. Feeling discouraged, she started to think that maybe she wasn't cut out to be a soldier.

Seeing that she was about to give up, Shang handed Mulan her horse's reins, and nodded at her approvingly. He was glad that this soldier was at last beginning to realize he did not belong in the army. Shoulders slumped in defeat, Mulan took the reins from him and turned to leave. Then, something inside her made her turn around and look at the pole again. At that moment she made a decision: she had to succeed! She had joined the army to save her father's life – and she would not give up.

Her brow furrowed in fierce determination, Mulan dropped the reins and marched over to the pole. She started to climb it and fell again. Then an idea came to her. Tying the bronze discs together, Mulan used their weight to help pull herself up the pole.

In awe, the rest of the men watched her shimmy up to the top. With her courage and determination, she had finally gained their trust and admiration. From now on, they would be proud to have this brave soldier as a member of their army.

The Beauty Within

Stories About Fairness and Judgment

Who Could Love a Beast?

from *Beauty and the Beast*

Sometimes a gruff exterior hides a tender heart.

To spare her father's life, Belle had promised to remain forever in the castle of a terrifying beast.

Belle had never intended to break her promise, even though it meant living with a creature whose monstrous features scared her. And the Beast seemed as ugly on the inside as the outside: he ordered her around and shouted at her constantly.

Unable to live with such an ill-tempered brute, Belle fled into the woods with her horse, Philippe. A pack of wolves started to chase after them. The wolves nipped at Philippe's heels, and Philippe reared up on his hind legs. Belle tumbled off his back and landed with a thump on the hard, frozen ground.

As the wolves closed in on her, Belle leaped up and grabbed a branch. Closer and closer the wolves crept, their yellow eyes shining and jagged teeth gleaming. Belle swept the branch back and forth. As she backed away from her attackers, she stumbled on a tangled root and fell. A wolf pounced on her and grazed her neck with its claws.

Suddenly someone yanked the wolf off her. It was the Beast. The wolves forgot about Belle and tackled the Beast, ripping his fur with their teeth and claws. Howling in pain, the Beast swung at them, trying to protect his eyes and face.

Gathering his strength, the Beast hurled one wolf after another away from him. When the other wolves saw that he could overpower them, they slunk away into the woods.

The Beast stumbled toward Belle, who had watched the fight helplessly. Suddenly he pitched forward and collapsed in the snow. The battle had weakened him, and his wounds were deep.

Belle looked down the path that led out of the forest. Now was her chance to escape. But the Beast had just saved her life. How could she abandon him now?

Belle turned to her horse and murmured, "Help me take him back, Philippe." She roused the Beast, then helped him to his feet. Using Philippe for support, Belle and the Beast made their way back to the castle.

Belle tended to the Beast's wounds, and he grew stronger each day. One morning the Beast surprised Belle by showing her a magnificent library.

"I can't believe it!" Belle exclaimed. "I've never seen so many books in my life!"

"You like it?" said the Beast. "It's all yours."

That afternoon, the Beast joined Belle outside and they played together in the snow. He even let Belle show him how to crouch down and feed the birds without scaring them off.

Belle was beginning to realize that she had been wrong about the Beast.

Quasimodo's Quick Thinking

from *The Hunchback of Notre Dame*

The humblest packages can contain the greatest gifts.

High above the city streets, Quasimodo watched the scene from the cathedral. Frollo, the wicked Minister of Justice, had sentenced the beautiful gypsy, Esmeralda, to death. Quasimodo knew that Frollo was capable of terrible things. After all, it had been Frollo who had banished the poor hunchbacked bell ringer to a life isolated from other people. Now Quasimodo feared for Esmeralda's life. He had to save her, but how? Frollo had locked him high in the cathedral bell tower.

The shouts of the crowd below grew louder and louder. Quasimodo paced anxiously back and forth, not sure what to do. Time was running out for Esmeralda. Quasimodo brushed past one of the heavy ropes for the bells and suddenly had an idea.

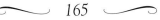

Quasimodo tied one end of a rope to a heavy gargoyle perched on the edge of the roof. Then, with a mighty shout, he leaped off, holding the other end of the rope. The wind whistled in his ears as he swooped down like an eagle. The rope swung right over Esmeralda. Quasimodo reached out and grabbed his friend, pulling her to safety.

"Get them!" shouted Frollo. He was furious that the hunchback had foiled his plans.

Quasimodo and Esmeralda escaped to the cathedral with Frollo's soldiers close behind. Soon the cathedral was surrounded, but Quasimodo was not ready to give up.

"Quick, this way!" he called to Esmeralda. They hurried to the bell tower. A huge pot of hot, liquid lead bubbled there. Quasimodo used the lead to repair cracks in the bells, but today it would serve a different purpose.

Together, Quasimodo and Esmeralda lifted the pot to a spot right above the soldiers. Hot steam rose into the air. With a nod to each other, they tilted the pot so that the hot lead poured out, down to where the soldiers were battering down the door.

"NO!" cried Frollo in frustration, as the soldiers dashed away from the boiling lead. His troops retreated as the crowd cheered for Quasimodo's quick thinking.

Quasimodo and Esmeralda looked down and heaved a sigh of relief. They were safe from Frollo and his men, thanks to Quasimodo, the hunchback of Notre Dame.

The Artist of Notre Dame

from *The Hunchback of Notre Dame*

—⚬⚬⚬—

Enemies' cruellest weapons can be words – don't let them hurt you.

The Festival of Fools was usually everyone's favourite holiday, but today was different. The evil Minister of Justice, Frollo, had ruined the day with his cruelty towards the gypsy dancer, Esmeralda. But she managed to escape Frollo by hiding in the Cathedral of Notre Dame.

Esmeralda was not the only one hiding in the cathedral that day. Quasimodo, the bell ringer, was there, too.

When Esmeralda called to him, he fled up the stone stairs to his home in the cathedral bell tower.

Esmeralda followed him. She was curious about this mysterious bell ringer.

At last they reached the loft where Quasimodo lived. A flock of pigeons flew over to greet Quasimodo. His friends – the gargoyles Victor, Hugo and Laverne, watched curiously. It was the first time Quasimodo had ever brought anyone to this place.

"Thank you for letting me stay here," Esmeralda said. Then she caught sight of a large table before her. On it was a miniature city of Paris carved of wood. Every building on every street was perfect. There were even people and horses and wagons.

"Did you make this?" Esmeralda asked softly. She lifted a delicate wooden figure of a dancing girl. It looked so much like her.

Quasimodo blushed. "I know it's not very good . . ." he started to answer.

Esmeralda took her friend's hand. "If I had talent like yours, I wouldn't need to dance in the street for a living," she told him.

"But your dancing is wonderful!" said Quasimodo. "It makes people happy! Everyone loves to watch you dance. But me – I'm a monster. Frollo told me so."

Esmeralda smiled. "Let me see your palm," she said, turning over Quasimodo's hand. Carefully she traced the lines in his palm with her fingertips. "Hmmmmm," she murmured.

"What is it?" Quasimodo asked nervously. No one had ever paid this much attention to him in his whole life.

Esmeralda pointed to a line on his hand. "See this? This line shows that you will live a long life. And this one tells me that you are shy." She hesitated. "But I don't see a single monster line."

Quasimodo stared at his palm as if it were the first time he had ever seen it. Could it be true? Had Frollo lied to him?

"Don't listen to Frollo," Esmeralda said seriously.

And suddenly, Quasimodo believed her.

Happy Birthday, Dumbo

from *Dumbo*

Often, it's the thing that makes you most different that makes you most special.

"He's perfect!" cried Mrs Jumbo, gazing proudly at her new baby. The other elephants crowded round.

"Isn't he adorable?" one of them cooed.

"Looks just like his mother," said another. All the elephants nodded in agreement.

Suddenly, the little elephant let out a big sneeze: "*Achooo!*" He shook his head and out flopped two enormous ears.

The elephants gasped. "Take a look at those ears!" one of them cried. "I never saw anything so dumb-looking in all my life. We'll have to call him Dumbo!"

The other elephants all laughed at poor Dumbo. He felt like crying.

Mrs Jumbo picked up her baby and stormed off to a corner so they could be alone.

"Don't pay any attention to them," she said. "I think you are the most handsome elephant in the world. They're just jealous."

Then she cuddled him and gently stroked him with her trunk until he fell fast asleep.

The next day, the circus train pulled into town. To announce their arrival, the animals paraded down the street in a long line. Dumbo was at the very end, holding tight to his mother's tail.

Dumbo was so excited that he forgot to look where he was going.

Flop! He tripped over his ears and fell right into a muddy puddle.

A little boy watching the parade laughed at him. "Look at those ears!" he shouted. "They'd make the biggest catapult in the world."

He ran up and pulled on Dumbo's ears. It hurt!

Dumbo's mother picked the boy up to teach him a lesson. He cried out, and some men dragged Mrs Jumbo away.

The other elephants told Dumbo it was all his fault his mother was gone. Poor Dumbo sat down by himself and began to cry. He was so lonely.

As he cried, he felt something tickle his trunk. It was a little mouse.

"Don't be sad, Dumbo," the mouse whispered. "I'm your friend. My name's Timothy."

Dumbo sniffed, and then he smiled. Suddenly he didn't feel quite so lonely any more.

Here Comes Hercules

from *Hercules*

Everyone makes mistakes sometimes.

ne day Hercules' father announced that he was going into town to sell some barley.

"Can I help, Dad?" the boy asked. Amphitryon hesitated for a moment. He knew that his son's incredible strength often caused problems. But he didn't want to disappoint the boy.

"Of course you can come," he said heartily.

When they reached the marketplace, Amphitryon instructed Hercules to watch over their load of barley. Then he went off to bargain with the merchants.

Nearby, some local boys were playing a game of discus. Hercules longed to join them, but when he asked if he could play, they refused.

"Good old Jerkules," they taunted. "Mr Destructo!"

If only they would give me a chance, thought Hercules sadly.

A moment later, his chance came. The discus sailed high above him. "I've got it!" he shouted.

Eager to show his skill and please the other boys, he leaped 30 feet into the air. But, instead of catching the discus, he smashed into one of the huge stone pillars that held up the marketplace roof. He crashed into it with such force that the pillar toppled. Then the whole roof came tumbling down and the merchants ran for their lives.

The townspeople were enraged. "Keep that crazy freak away from here!" they yelled. "He's dangerous!"

"He's just a kid," Amphitryon pleaded, hoping they'd understand. "He can't control his strength."

"Get him out of here!" chanted the townspeople. "He's a freak, freak, freak!"

Hercules was crushed. He hadn't meant any harm. He was silent all the way home.

"Son, don't let those people get to you," Amphitryon finally said.

Hercules hung his head. He knew his father was right, but he didn't feel any better.

One day, he thought to himself, *I'll show them. One day I'll find a place where I belong.*

Esmeralda's Escape

from *The Hunchback of Notre Dame*

Justice is colour-blind. Judge people by their actions, not their appearance.

he Festival of Fools was a day filled with merriment and joy. Everyone in Paris came out to celebrate with singing and dancing, including the gypsies. And the best of all the gypsy dancers was the beautiful Esmeralda.

Esmeralda smiled at her little goat friend, Djali. She loved the Festival of Fools, not only for the joy it brought, but also for the money she could earn dancing. There were not many ways a gypsy could make a living. Esmeralda danced in the street, jingling her tambourine, and people would toss her a few coins if they enjoyed watching her. The Festival of Fools seemed to bring out the generosity in everybody.

"This looks like a good spot, Djali," she said. She looked up and down the street. Almost everyone would have to pass this way on their way to the cathedral.

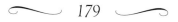

Esmeralda held her tambourine high over her head and gave it a shake. She dipped her head down slowly, and then straightened up, shaking the tambourine. Then she began to dance, swirling and spinning so that her bright peasant skirt twirled in a circle. The people who passed stopped to admire the lovely young dancer, and almost everyone was happy to throw a few coins into her hat.

One of the men who stopped was Phoebus, a soldier. He was enchanted by Esmeralda. He was about to speak to her when two soldiers suddenly interrupted the dance.

"Where did you get this money, gypsy?" they sneered at Esmeralda.

Esmeralda folded her arms. "For your information, I earned it!" she said angrily.

"Ha!" the soldiers said. "Everyone knows you gypsies are nothing but thieves!"

With that, the soldiers grabbed Esmeralda's hat to take her money. Coins flew into the street. Djali quickly came to his friend's aid by butting the soldiers with his hard little head.

"Get her!" the soldiers cried as Esmeralda dashed away.

Phoebus knew Esmeralda had done nothing wrong. Just as the soldiers were about to run past him, he led his horse, Achilles, into their path. The soldiers fell with a *splat* in a puddle.

"Achilles, sit!" Phoebus commanded. The horse sat . . . right on one of the soldiers!

The soldier spluttered furiously. Phoebus watched as Esmeralda disappeared down the street. No matter what anyone said about gypsies, he had seen for himself that Esmeralda was no thief. He was glad he had helped her, and hoped he would see her again soon.

Dawson's Detective Work

from *The Great Mouse Detective*

'Good job' is one of the nicest things you can hear or say.

ight had fallen on the city. Olivia and Dawson were still at the house of Basil, the great mouse detective, wondering how to rescue Olivia's father, who had been kidnapped. They all suspected Ratigan, but they agreed that nothing could be done without first getting some evidence against him.

"Watch out!" Olivia cried. She had caught a glimpse of Ratigan's evil sidekick, Fidget, outside Basil's window. Fortunately the bat had not spotted her. "He was looking in the window, and then he turned away and ran off!"

"What a stroke of luck!" Basil exclaimed. "Come, Dawson, Olivia! Let's go outside and look for footprints."

Basil was right. Fidget had left many dirty footprints on the pavement. "We can't mistake Fidget's footprints because of his wooden leg," Basil explained.

But rain began to fall, and one by one the footprints disappeared.

Dawson had found something lying on the ground. It was a cap.

"Look here!" he shouted, waving the cap in the air.

"That must be Fidget's cap!" Basil cried. "He most likely dropped it as he walked."

The detective examined the cap and nodded with satisfaction.

"Good work, Dawson!" he said. "It's just the piece of evidence we need. I think I'll make you a partner, my friend!"

Dawson smiled. "At your service!" He felt very proud.

Friendship Blooms

from *Bambi*

───────⚬⚬⚬⚬⚬───────

A few kind words can change everything.

Bambi, a newborn fawn, was curious about everything. His friend Thumper, a young rabbit, was eager to show him the world. Wherever Bambi went in the forest, animals greeted him. "Good morning, young prince!" they called.

Suddenly a small golden creature danced before Bambi's eyes. Startled, Bambi watched it flit about. He chased the creature as it darted ahead. Finally, it landed on Bambi's tail.

"Bird!" proclaimed Bambi.

Thumper had introduced him to a bird only moments before.

"No, that's not a bird," Thumper said. "That's a *butterfly*."

"Butterfly?" Bambi whispered to himself. There were so many words to learn.

Bambi turned to look at the butterfly again, but it had flown away. He looked around, and thought he'd found it.

"Butterfly!" he cried at a golden, soft thing on the ground. He was *sure* it was a butterfly!

But Thumper laughed. "No, that's a *flower*!"

"Flower," said Bambi, tasting the word.

"Uh-huh," said Thumper, showing Bambi how to sniff one. "It's *pretty*," he said.

"Pretty," Bambi repeated, and he bent again to the flower patch, sniffing deeply. A lovely, sweet scent filled his nostrils and tingled through his whole body. What a wonderful new sensation!

Suddenly one of the flowers twitched, and Bambi's nose touched the nose of a young skunk.

"Flower!" cried Bambi happily to the black-and-white creature.

"Me?" said the skunk in surprise. No one had ever called him a flower before.

Thumper burst out laughing. Imagine calling something as stinky as a skunk a flower!

"No, no, no!" Thumper cried, correcting Bambi. "That's not a flower. He's a little–"

The skunk cut him off. "Oh, that's all right," the skunk said. "He can call me a flower if he wants to!" The skunk giggled. "I don't mind a bit!"

The skunk had never felt so warm and happy inside. He was a shy animal, and used to being shunned by strangers.

"Pretty, pretty flower!" Bambi exclaimed.

"Oh, gosh," said the skunk, and he laughed softly.

From then on, Bambi, Thumper and Flower were the best of friends.

Journeys of Discovery

Stories About Happiness

Soaring Through the Stars

from *Aladdin*

The world is a magical place. Choose your own adventure!

ong ago, in the kingdom of Agrabah, the Sultan wanted to make sure that his only daughter would always be cared for, so he insisted on following the law that said the Princess must marry a prince before her 16th birthday.

Princess Jasmine had only three days left in which to choose a husband. One after another, princes journeyed to the palace, and one after another, the princes were sent away, because Jasmine thought they were conceited or pompous or just plain dull.

Prince Ali Ababwa seemed to be the worst of all. Jasmine had actually overheard him say to the Sultan, "Just let her meet me. *I* will win your daughter!"

That night, as Jasmine paced in her room, the Prince appeared on her balcony.

"Please, Princess, give me a chance!" cried Prince Ali, who was really the street urchin Aladdin.

Jasmine frowned. There was something familiar about the Prince's voice and eyes. "Do I know you?" she asked. "You remind me of someone I met in the marketplace."

"Marketplace?" he repeated in shock. "*I* would never go there." He was trying to behave as he imagined a prince would.

From his snobbish response, it became clear to Jasmine that he was just another swaggering peacock. Finally, in exasperation, Jasmine cried, "Go and jump off a balcony!"

As the Prince turned to leave, he conceded, "You aren't just a prize to be won. You should be free to make your own choice."

Jasmine watched Prince Ali step off the balcony. Instead of falling, he seemed to float. "How are you doing that?" she asked.

"It's a magic carpet," Aladdin replied. "You don't want to go for a ride, do you? We could go away and see the world. . . ."

"Is it safe?" Jasmine asked, eyeing the carpet.

"Sure," Aladdin replied, holding out his hand. "Do you trust me?"

"Yes," said Jasmine, stepping onto the carpet. Now she was almost certain that Prince Ali was the boy in the marketplace. The boy had used the same expression:

Do you trust me?

The carpet flew over the twinkling lights of Agrabah, and sailed over the starlit desert. It drifted over the dark and rolling sea.

Jasmine held on tight, enjoying every moment. She gasped as they

zoomed past the pyramids of Egypt. She laughed as they dipped down into an apple orchard and Prince Ali plucked an apple off a tree. She caught her breath as they set down in China and watched a fireworks display from the roof of a pagoda.

Soon Jasmine would find out more about this so-called prince. But whatever happened, she would never forget her magical tour of the big, wonderful, surprising world.

A Slippery Situation

from *Bambi*

Learning can be full of ups and downs — keep trying.

One morning Bambi awoke to find that the ground had changed colour. It was no longer dark and covered with twigs and dried leaves. Something miraculous had happened overnight.

"Mother, look!" Bambi cried. "What's all that white stuff?"

"Why, it's snow," she explained calmly.

"Snow?" asked Bambi.

"Yes," his mother replied. "Winter has come."

Bambi ventured out of the thicket. Each time Bambi stepped on the snow, his hoof sank into the soft white powder. When he lifted his hoof, it left a hole.

As Bambi explored the cold, snowy forest, he found his friend Thumper playing by the pond.

"Look, Bambi," said Thumper. "Watch what I can do."

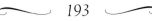

Thumper ran down a snowbank and leaped into the air, then slid on his behind across the pond. "Whee!" cried Thumper.

Bambi didn't understand why Thumper didn't sink to the bottom of the pond. But then Thumper thumped his foot on the hard surface. "Look," he said to Bambi. "The water's stiff!"

Bambi could tell that Thumper was having fun. Maybe he could slide across the pond, too. Like Thumper, Bambi ran down the snowbank and leaped onto the ice. Bambi expected to glide across the surface, but his legs slipped out from under him, and he spun around on his tummy.

Thumper skated up to him. "Some fun, huh, Bambi?" said the little rabbit.

Bambi didn't know what to say. His slippery little hooves and spindly legs didn't seem to work the way Thumper's short legs and long, flat feet did.

But maybe Bambi just needed more practice. He tried to stand, but all four hooves slipped out from under him again.

"A little wobbly, aren't you?" said Thumper as he tried to push Bambi's legs into position.

Finally, Thumper helped Bambi stand up. Thumper pushed Bambi, and Bambi started to glide. Then Bambi's back legs twisted beneath him, and he tumbled to the ice again.

"You have to watch both ends at the same time," Thumper said. He helped Bambi up and pushed him again.

This time, it was a much bigger push, and Bambi sailed across the ice – faster and faster, until he slipped again. Bambi slid on his stomach and bumped into Thumper. Together they slid and slid, until they crashed into a snowbank.

Bambi sat up in the soft snow and looked around excitedly. He wondered what he would learn next!

Double Trouble

from *The Prince and the Pauper*

Don't be too quick to trade your troubles away.

 ne day, a hungry pauper chased his dog, Pluto, through the castle gates. His friend Goofy, who was also very poor, stood outside and watched helplessly as the Captain of the Guard grabbed Mickey and dragged him up to the Prince's chamber.

The Prince and Mickey gasped at the sight of one another.

"Gosh, Your Royal Highness," said Mickey. "We could be twins!" Mickey bowed low and introduced himself.

"I was about to die of boredom when you interrupted my lesson," said the Prince. "Do you know what it's like to be the Prince?"

"It must be fun!" said Mickey.

"Breakfast at seven. Lessons until lunch. Fencing until tea time. A banquet every night. How I envy your freedom!"

"You envy *me?*" said Mickey, amazed.

"Sure I do," continued the Prince. "You don't have to study dreary books. You can stay up as late as you like . . . " Suddenly he perked up. "You've given me a wonderful idea! We'll change places for a day! Nobody will be able to tell the difference."

And so it was done.

Soon, the Prince found that living in the streets wasn't as easy as he had thought. He discovered that his own guards stole food from the starving people. And he himself was accused of stealing. He was lucky to have a friend like Goofy, who let him hide in his house.

Inside the castle, Mickey was having a hard time, as well. His lessons were indeed boring, and his schedule was exhausting. And worst of all, he was hustled upstairs to hear the last words of the King, who was dying.

"My son," the King said to the nervous Mickey, "soon you will be King. You must promise that you will rule the land justly, and with compassion for all."

Mickey promised. As he hurried to find the Prince, the Captain of the Guard seized him. "Good day, my phony Prince," said the Captain. "Now that our dear departed King is out of the way, you're going to do everything I say, because if you don't, your little doggie, Pluto, will pay for it!"

That night, the Captain found the Prince in Goofy's house. He hauled the Prince back into the castle and tossed him in the dungeon. "After the pauper's crowned," said the Captain, "it will be bye-bye for you!"

The Prince slumped to the floor. If only he hadn't wanted to change places with Mickey!

Just then Goofy appeared with the key to the cell. It had fallen out of the Captain's pocket, and Goofy had snatched it up.

The Prince joined Mickey moments before the coronation. The Captain's plan was revealed and he was hauled off to prison. The Prince became King. And from that day on, he ruled with justice and compassion . . . with Mickey as his trusted advisor.

A Mad Tea Party

from *Alice in Wonderland*

—⟨≈≈⟩—

Good manners are a welcome addition to any party.

lice found the March Hare and the Mad Hatter sitting at one end of a long table in the middle of the woods. The two friends were singing and having a grand old time.

"How curious," Alice said to herself. As they sang and danced about, only occasionally did any tea land in one of the many pretty cups that were strewn about the table.

Not wishing to be rude, Alice sat down at the other end of the table and waited for an opportunity to politely introduce herself.

All of a sudden, the March Hare and the Mad Hatter took notice of Alice. They stopped singing and swooped down on her, crying, "No room! No room! Sorry, all filled up!"

Alice was quite taken aback. "But there's plenty of room!" she declared, peering down the length of the long, empty table.

"Oh, but it's very rude to sit down without being invited," the March Hare informed her.

"I'll say," the Mad Hatter declared. "It's very, very rude."

"Very, very, very rude indeed," the Dormouse agreed, popping his head out of a teapot, where he'd been napping.

"I'm very sorry," said Alice, "but I did so enjoy your singing and I –"

"You enjoyed our singing?" cried the March Hare.

"Oh, what a delightful child!" beamed the Mad Hatter, dunking his elbow into a full cup. "You must stay and have some tea."

"That would be nice," Alice replied, thinking she'd never been to such an odd tea party in all her life.

But no sooner had Alice raised the cup to her lips than the Mad Hatter snatched it away, crying, "Clean cup!" and "Move down!"

"But I haven't used this one," cried Alice as the March Hare shoved her out of her chair.

When she was settled in her new place, Alice began to ask if either of them had seen the White Rabbit. But the Mad Hatter immediately interrupted her. "Don't you care for tea?" he asked, pouring it straight from the pot down his throat.

"Why, yes, I'm very fond of tea," said Alice, who had yet to swallow a sip, "but –"

"If you don't care for tea," the March Hare broke in, "you could at least make polite conversation."

"Well," spluttered Alice, "I've been trying to ask you –"

"I have an excellent idea," said the March Hare. "Let's change the subject. How about a nice cup of tea?"

"A cup of tea, indeed!" Alice cried. "You're mad – all of you!"

And with that, she stormed off into the woods to find the White Rabbit.

Aurora's Birthday Lesson

from *Sleeping Beauty*

Sometimes the right thing is the hardest thing to do.

The three good fairies were very excited. They had cared for the Princess Aurora for 16 years, keeping her hidden safe in the forest from the wicked Maleficent. In order to make sure their secret was secure, they even changed Aurora's name to Briar Rose, and gave up their magic wands to live as humans.

But today was Briar Rose's 16th birthday. The fairies would return her to the castle at sunset.

"I'm going to miss Briar Rose," Flora said with a sniff.

"There, there, dearie," said Merryweather, patting her on the shoulder. "We all will."

"It seems like only yesterday that we brought her here as a baby," sighed Fauna.

The fairies fell silent. They loved Briar Rose as though she were their own daughter. Saying goodbye was going to be difficult.

"I know!" cried Flora suddenly. "Let's celebrate her birthday here, before we bring her back to the castle. It will be our special way of saying goodbye."

Fauna and Merryweather thought that was a wonderful idea.

"I'll make a cake!" said Fauna, rolling up her sleeves.

"Have you ever made a cake before, dear?" asked Merryweather sweetly. The truth was, none of the fairies was very good at doing things without using magic.

"We'll make her a dress, too," said Flora. "We want her to look pretty when the King and Queen see her. They've waited such a long time for her to come home."

The fairies set to work at once. Soon the cottage was dusty with flour and sugar, and eggshells crunched underfoot as Fauna did her best with the cake recipe. Merryweather and Flora argued about the dress.

"It should be pink!"

"Oh, no, dearie. It must be blue!"

"This is ridiculous!" said Flora finally. "We should be thinking about what will make Briar Rose happy. I'm getting my wand."

"Me, too!" cried the others. Soon the cake was magically made and a stunning dress hung from a door.

Just then, Briar Rose came home. She was overjoyed to see the trouble her dear aunts had taken for her. But her joy was short-lived when she learned that she would be leaving her home in the forest.

"It's for the best, dearie," explained Merryweather gently.

Briar Rose knew her aunts hated her to go as much as she hated going. But she understood that her place was at the castle now. Just as they had done the right thing for the last 16 years, now it was right for her to take her place as the Princess of the land.

Kittens in the Kitchen

from *Three Orphan Kittens*

⟨⟨⟨⟨⟨

Happiness is often found where you least expect it.

 ne day, three little kittens were born in a barn: one black, one white and one tortoiseshell. Although the kittens loved one another, the farmer who owned them did not love them. So the farmer's son decided to take them into town, where he hoped to find them a new home. During the ride, the truck hit a bump, and the kittens tumbled into the snow.

The kittens wandered across the countryside until they found a farmhouse. Creeping softly through an open cellar door, they found a

bright, warm kitchen filled with wonderful cooking smells. On the floor rested a big saucer of milk. Hungrily, the kittens lapped up the delicious milk, splattering it all over their faces. They crawled under the stove and, as they carefully groomed themselves, they heard footsteps. From their hiding place, the kittens could see two great big feet. The feet stopped at the table, then walked away.

The kittens scampered up the side of the tablecloth onto the table. There they discovered a freshly baked, sweet-smelling cherry pie.

The black kitten pounced into the middle of the pie, squirting juice at the other kittens. When he crawled out of the pie, the white kitten and the tortoiseshell kitten pinned him down and licked all the cherry juice off his fur.

All clean, the black kitten pounced too close to the edge of the table and slipped, pulling the tablecloth down. Plates and silverware clattered to the floor, and the cherry pie landed on top of the black kitten. More cherries and cherry juice for everyone to enjoy!

After the kittens had licked themselves clean, they set out to explore the rest of the house. In the dining room, they batted a feather around. Then they climbed up on a piano and danced on the keys.

Suddenly they heard the two big feet clomping across the floor. The kittens jumped off the piano, and the big feet chased the kittens all over the house.

Frightened, they raced upstairs and dashed into a little girl's bedroom. In the wardrobe, each kitten found a shoe to snuggle in. Soon they were fast asleep.

The next morning, the little girl found them. Delighted, she cuddled the kittens in her arms and promised to love them forever.

Belle's Books

from *Beauty and the Beast*

Sometimes the most exciting place to be is in the middle of a book.

henever Belle came to town, the people there began to whisper among themselves.

"There goes Belle, the inventor's daughter," they said. "She's beautiful, but so . . . different."

Belle was different. Other people were happy to spend their whole lives in the tiny town, seeing the same faces every day, doing the same things from one year to the next. Not Belle. She dreamed of romance, adventure and a life beyond her little world.

No matter how busy she was, Belle always stopped at the bookshop whenever she came to town.

"Good morning!" she called as the doorbell rang merrily.

The bookshop owner smiled. Not many people in town loved books the way Belle did, and he was always glad to see her.

"I have some new books today, Belle," he told her. Her face lit up.

"Adventures?" she asked breathlessly. "Love stories? Fairy tales?"

"All three," the shopkeeper replied, piling her arms with books. Then he winked. "And don't finish them all in one day this time, or you won't have anything to read tomorrow!"

Belle laughed. "That's all right. I'll just read them all over again!"

The books were heavy as she walked out of the shop, but Belle didn't mind. Then Gaston reached for one of them.

Gaston knew nothing about books. All he cared about was himself.

"Why do you waste your time *reading?*" he asked Belle. "You could be spending more time with me."

Belle quickly took her book and got away from him. At last she sat down and opened the biggest book. With Gaston gone and sheep grazing on some flowers nearby, Belle was finally able to begin her story.

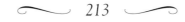

"Once upon a time, in a faraway land," she read, "a handsome prince was trapped in a fairy's spell . . . " Belle sighed happily. This was just the kind of book she loved. Sometimes she couldn't wait to see how a story ended, and tried to guess what would happen right from the beginning.

Belle didn't have much time to wonder about it, though, for at that moment, an explosion came from her house.

"Oh, Papa!" she sighed, closing her book. "I guess my adventure with a handsome prince is going to have to wait!" And with a wave goodbye to the sheep, she headed for home.

The Aristocats' Adventure

from *The Aristocats*

There are times when you have to be lost before you can find a new road.

Duchess and her kittens, Toulouse, Berlioz and Marie, were aristocats. That meant that they had very fine manners and lived a comfortable life in an elegant house in Paris. Madame, their owner, loved them very much, and her butler Edgar had to make sure that their every need was taken care of. Edgar always did as he was asked but, deep down, he was very jealous of the cats.

One night Edgar overheard Madame telling her lawyer that she was planning to leave her entire fortune to her pets. Edgar was furious. He wanted that money for himself! He knew he had to act fast. That night, Edgar kidnapped the aristocats and abandoned them in the country.

"Where are we, Mama?" Marie asked, shivering in the cold.

Duchess looked around. The countryside was very different from the busy city she was used to. All she could see were trees and grass and a blue sky. She heard birds chirping and a stream bubbling. Then she heard something else. It was a big alley cat singing!

The cat stopped singing and stared when he saw Duchess. He had never seen such a beautiful cat before. His name was O'Malley, and

when he met the kittens, he knew he had to help. Soon the cats were
on their way back to the city.

Paris was very far away, but with O'Malley, the trip was an
adventure. The cats climbed aboard a milk truck for a ride, then
pretended to be a train when they came to some train tracks. And it
was very exciting when Marie fell in the river and O'Malley bravely
rescued her. By the end of the day, the little ones were very tired from
all they had done.

"We'd better stop for the night," O'Malley told Duchess. "I have a
pad right over there. It isn't fancy, but it's nice and quiet."

Just then a loud blast from a trumpet burst from the window of
O'Malley's pad. His alley-cat friends had come by, and were having a
party.

"These cats really know how to swing!" O'Malley told Duchess.

Duchess loved Thomas's friends. They played music and sang and danced until the kittens couldn't keep their eyes open any more. At last, the party ended.

"I think Mama likes Mr O'Malley," the kittens whispered sleepily to each other.

Duchess did like O'Malley. He had shown her a life she had never known before. He was not an aristocat, but that didn't bother her. He was clever, brave, funny and very kind. Duchess knew that with him by her side, she and her kittens would have nothing to fear.

Grandmother Willow's Wisdom

from *Pocahontas*

Listen to others' advice. Then let your heart be your guide.

Pocahontas pushed her canoe into the river. Her raccoon friend, Meeko, hopped in, and Flit the bird flew alongside them as they went, not wanting to be left behind.

Pocahontas paddled till she came to a hidden stream. She entered a part of the forest that was cool and green, humming with peace and life. In the heart of it, she came to Grandmother Willow, a tree that had stood there for hundreds of years. Grandmother Willow's knowledge of the earth ran deep.

Pocahontas climbed out of her canoe and knelt at Grandmother Willow's roots.

"Grandmother Willow," she said softly. "I need your help."

The bark of the ancient tree began to change shape. Soon Pocahontas saw the face of a kind old woman appear.

"Good morning, child," said Grandmother Willow, her rich voice filling the air. "I was hoping you'd visit today. Now tell me – what's troubling you?"

Pocahontas sighed. "My father wishes me to marry Kocoum."

"Kocoum?" asked Grandmother Willow. She frowned. "But he's so . . . serious."

"Exactly," said Pocahontas. "And there's another thing. Lately I've been having the strangest dream."

"Oh, good!" Grandmother Willow laughed. "You know how I love dreams. Tell me all about it."

"I dream," Pocahontas began, "that I'm running through the woods. Then, right there before me, is an arrow. As I look at it, it begins to spin."

"A spinning arrow!" Grandmother Willow murmured. "How unusual."

"Yes!" cried Pocahontas. "And it spins faster and faster – until suddenly it stops."

"And then?" asked Grandmother Willow.

Pocahontas shrugged. "And then I wake up."

Grandmother was silent for a long time, pondering the meaning of the dream.

Finally Grandmother Willow spoke.

"Child," she said. "It seems to me this spinning arrow is pointing you down your path – the path your life should take."

"I know," said Pocahontas. "But what is my path? How am I going to find it?"

Grandmother Willow chuckled softly.

"Your mother asked me the very same question," she said.

"And what did you tell her?" Pocahontas demanded.

"I told her to listen. Spirits are all around you, child. They live in the earth, the water, the sky. Listen to them, and they will show you where to go."

The playful breeze rustled through Grandmother Willow's leaves once again.

"Wait! I can hear the wind," said Pocahontas, straining to hear a hidden message.

"What is it telling you?" asked Grandmother Willow.

Pocahontas listened harder. "I don't know," she sighed.

"Now, now, child," Grandmother Willow said. "Don't give up yet. There are more ways than one to listen. You must listen with your heart as well as your ears. Then you will understand."

Pocahontas closed her eyes and listened again.

This time, she heard a voice. Her eyes flew open.

"The wind is saying something!"

Grandmother Willow smiled. Pocahontas listened to the voice, which told her to climb the huge tree and look out. When she did, she saw strange clouds – clouds that were the sails of a ship from England. And on that ship was John Smith, the man Pocahontas would soon meet – and come to love.

A Dutiful Daughter

from *Mulan*

Be true to your own dreams – not someone else's.

Five young women in the Chinese village were gathered together, waiting for the Matchmaker to look them over. Each looked like a porcelain doll – bathed, made up and dressed to perfection.

Mulan was among them, hoping against hope that she would remember to do and say the right things. She did not want to be there, but she did want to bring honour to her family.

"Fa Mulan!" the Matchmaker barked. Mulan stepped inside the

Matchmaker's pavilion while her mother and grandmother looked on. They were as nervous as Mulan, for they knew how hard it was for the high-spirited girl to be demure and ladylike. And the Matchmaker was *not* a very understanding woman.

Mulan stood silently, trying not to fidget as the Matchmaker circled around her. "Too skinny!" the Matchmaker growled. "Not good for bearing sons."

At that moment, Cri-kee the cricket jumped onto Mulan's shoulder. Mulan grabbed him and tossed him away. But he wouldn't leave! He hopped back onto Mulan's shoulder, and then onto her head. Mulan quickly popped Cri-Kee in her mouth to hide him.

"Recite the final admonition," the Matchmaker demanded.

Mulan couldn't – her mouth was full. Thinking quickly, she

opened her fan and spat out Cri-Kee. She cleared her throat. "Fulfil your duties calmly and . . . " what was the next line? " . . . respectfully. Reflect before you snack – I mean *act*!"

The Matchmaker looked suspicious.

"This shall bring you honour and glory," Mulan concluded, relieved.

The Matchmaker grabbed Mulan by the arm and led her to a tea table. "Now, pour the tea," she ordered. "To please your future in-laws, you must demonstrate a sense of dignity and refinement. You must also be poised."

Suddenly, Cri-Kee jumped down the Matchmaker's dress. Mulan was so shocked that she poured tea on the Matchmaker.

"Why, you clumsy –" the Matchmaker got up too quickly and knocked over the incense burner. Her dress caught fire.

"Put it out! Put it out!" she yelled. Mulan doused her with the entire pot of tea.

The Matchmaker, steaming with fury, turned to Mulan. "You are a disgrace. You may look like a bride, but you will never bring honour to your family!" she snarled.

That afternoon, Mulan was filled with shame. But she had hope, too. One day she would surely bloom into her true self.

The Mancub Meets His Match

from *The Jungle Book*

Be happy. Be strong. Belong.

The last place Mowgli wanted to go was the Man-village. He had been raised by wolves, and he was perfectly content to live among his animal friends in the jungle. The thought of the Man-village – filled with things and creatures he'd never seen – terrified him.

But the wise panther, Bagheera, knew that it was time for the mancub to return to his own kind. He was afraid that the cruel tiger, Shere Khan, would hurt the little boy he had come to love.

While the panther tried to guide Mowgli to the Man-village, the wild little boy resisted with all his might. But suddenly Mowgli heard a sweet sound. It was the sound of someone singing – a human someone. Mowgli was enchanted. He had never heard anything so beautiful. He ran to find the source of the voice, and stopped dead in his tracks.

"What's that?" he demanded.

"It's the Man-village," answered Bagheera, as they finally came to some man-made dwellings.

"No, I mean that," said Mowgli, pointing to a pretty little girl. She was filling a jug with water from the river, and it was she who had been singing.

"I want to take a closer look," Mowgli said. "I've never seen one before. I'll be right back!"

He ran toward the girl.

Bagheera watched as Mowgli climbed a tree overlooking the river. Suddenly, the branch broke and Mowgli went tumbling into the shallow water. The girl's eyes opened wide in surprise, but when she saw Mowgli splashing about she put her hand over her mouth and giggled. Mowgli ran to hide in the bushes, but he peeked out shyly and smiled.

Finally, Mowgli summoned the courage to come out of hiding. The girl giggled again and started to walk towards the village, balancing the jug of water on her head. Suddenly she dropped the jug, and the water spilled on the ground. The jug rolled over to Mowgli.

Mowgli picked it up and ran to refill it. Then he placed the jug on his head, just as he had seen the girl do. He turned once and looked back at Bagheera. The mancub shrugged and smiled. Waving goodbye, he followed the girl to the Man-village.

Cinderella's Surprise

from *Cinderella*

Doing a good deed is a gift you can give to yourself.

very morning, the rays of the sun shone into Cinderella's room. Little birds flew in at her window, chirping for her to wake up.

"Good morning!" Cinderella sang to them.

The birds flew around the shabby room, helping Cinderella get dressed. The didn't care that her dress was patched and old. They loved her because she was always so cheerful and kind.

Cinderella loved her feathered friends, too. Her stepmother and stepsisters treated her so poorly that the only joy she had was the happy birds' singing. That and her dreams.

There was no time for dreaming this morning, though. The birds had an important message for Cinderella.

"What?" Cinderella asked, trying to understand them. "A mouse is caught in a trap? Oh, the poor thing!"

Cinderella ran down the stairs. A mouse was trembling in the back of the rat trap.

Gently, Cinderella set the mouse free. "I'll call you Gus," she decided.

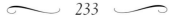

Gus quickly realized that Cinderella was his friend. She gave him his own little jumper and hat and all the corn he could carry.

"Now, Jacques, take care of Gus," she told a skinny mouse. "And don't forget to warn him about the cat!"

Cinderella hummed as she did her daily chores. In her mind, she was far away, dancing with her true love. A knock on the door brought her out of her daydreams.

"A message from the King!" announced the courier. Cinderella quickly took her the message to her stepmother.

"There's to be a ball!" exclaimed her stepmother. "And every young maiden in the land is invited! Of course, you will need to wear something suitable."

The stepsisters squealed. Before long, Cinderella found herself busy sewing and ironing beautiful ball gowns for them. There was no time to make a dress for herself.

"Poor Cinderelly," sighed Jacques. "She never gets to have any fun."

"She's always helped us. Now we can help her!" chirped the birds suddenly. "We'll make a dress for her so she can go, too!"

The animals scurried about with bits of ribbon and lace and thread. That evening, a very tired and sad Cinderella opened the door to her tiny room.

"Surprise!" shouted the animals. There was the most beautiful ball gown awaiting her. Cinderella's face lit up. Her friends were delighted. They had helped make their favourite person's dream come true.

A Silly Celebration

from *Alice in Wonderland*

———✣———

You can always find something to celebrate.

hile looking for the March Hare, Alice came upon him and the Mad Hatter, drinking tea at a long, beautifully decorated table, surrounded by a picket fence. She sat down at their table and they offered her some tea. She accepted happily, trying to ignore the fact that they were spilling more tea than they were pouring.

"I'm sorry I interrupted your birthday party," she said politely.

"Birthday?" the March Hare snorted. "My dear child, this is not a birthday party!

"This is an *un*birthday party!" the Mad Hatter chimed in. When Alice just looked at him blankly, he went on to explain why unbirthdays were so much better than birthdays. With everyone getting just one birthday each year, the March Hare pointed out, that left 364 unbirthdays to celebrate. And that is just what the Mad Hatter and the March Hare were doing.

Alice considered the idea for a moment, then laughed out loud. "Why, then today is my unbirthday, too!" she announced happily.

"It is?" the Mad Hatter said. "What a small world!" Tipping his hat in honour of Alice, he removed from under it a lovely unbirthday cake, which he presented to her with a flourish.

While Alice admired her cake, the Mad Hatter and the March Hare joined hands and danced around her, singing a very merry unbirthday song.

"Now blow out the candle, my dear," said the Mad Hatter.

Alice made a wish, and then blew as hard as she could. *Whoosh!* For a moment the golden flame on the candle sizzled and fizzled. Then, like a rocket, the cake blasted off and zoomed high into the sky. Alice gasped as a dazzling explosion of fireworks rained down all around her.

It was all so strange and wonderful. Alice loved every minute of the unbirthday party. And to think – she had 363 more unbirthdays to celebrate that year!